THE ONLY LIVING WITNESS

"Slick, how come we got to chase this broad all over the Wild West? She's run away scared to death. She knows what'll happen to her if she ever shows her face back in St. Louis. She ain't going to talk. Why can't we just forget her and go on back to the city?"

"Listen, dummy," Slick said. "She saw me do the deed. Yeah, she's running right now, but what happens when she gets tired of running? When she runs out of dough? All her bank accounts are back there. She'll have to come back. And if we quit looking for her, the cops won't. They know she's the only witness. If we don't get to her first, they'll find her, one of these days, and bring her back. And there ain't no statute of limitations on murder."

DON'T MISS THESE ALL-ACTION WESTERN SERIES FROM THE BERKLEY PUBLISHING GROUP

THE GUNSMITH by J. R. Roberts

Clint Adams was a legend among lawmen, outlaws, and ladies. They called him . . . the Gunsmith.

LONGARM by Tabor Evans

The popular long-running series about Deputy U.S. Marshal Long—his life, his loves, his fight for justice.

SLOCUM by Jake Logan

Today's longest-running action Western. John Slocum rides a deadly trail of hot blood and cold steel.

BUSHWHACKERS by B. J. Lanagan

An action-packed series by the creators of Longarm! The rousing adventures of the most brutal gang of cutthroats ever assembled—Quantrill's Raiders.

DIAMONDBACK by Guy Brewer

Dex Yancey is Diamondback, a Southern gentleman turned con man when his brother cheats him out of the family fortune. Ladies love him. Gamblers hate him. But nobody pulls one over on Dex . . .

WILDGUN by Jack Hanson

The blazing adventures of mountain man Will Barlow—from the creators of Longarm!

TEXAS TRACKER by Tom Calhoun

Meet J.T. Law: the most relentless—and dangerous—manhunter in all Texas. Where sheriffs and posses fail, he's the best man to bring in the most vicious outlaws—for a price.

JAKE LOGAN

SLOCUM AND THE CITY SLICKERS

JOVE BOOKS, NEW YORK

THE BERKLEY PUBLISHING GROUP
Published by the Penguin Group
Penguin Group (USA) Inc.
375 Hudson Street, New York, New York 10014, USA
Penguin Group (Canada), 90 Eglinton Avenue East, Suite 700, Toronto, Ontario M4P 2Y3, Canada
(a division of Pearson Penguin Canada Inc.)
Penguin Books Ltd., 80 Strand, London WC2R 0RL, England
Penguin Group Ireland, 25 St. Stephen's Green, Dublin 2, Ireland (a division of Penguin Books Ltd.)
Penguin Group (Australia), 250 Camberwell Road, Camberwell, Victoria 3124, Australia
(a division of Pearson Australia Group Pty. Ltd.)
Penguin Books India Pvt. Ltd., 11 Community Centre, Panchsheel Park, New Delhi—110 017, India
Penguin Group (NZ), 67 Apollo Drive, Mairangi Bay, Auckland 1311, New Zealand
(a division of Pearson New Zealand Ltd.)
Penguin Books (South Africa) (Pty.) Ltd., 24 Sturdee Avenue, Rosebank, Johannesburg 2196,
South Africa

Penguin Books Ltd., Registered Offices: 80 Strand, London WC2R 0RL, England

SLOCUM AND THE CITY SLICKERS

A Jove Book / published by arrangement with the author

PRINTING HISTORY
Jove edition / June 2007

For information, address: The Berkley Publishing Group,
a division of Penguin Group (USA) Inc.,
375 Hudson Street, New York, New York 10014.

ISBN: 978-0-515-14309-6

JOVE®
Jove Books are published by The Berkley Publishing Group,
a division of Penguin Group (USA) Inc.
375 Hudson Street, New York, New York 10014.
JOVE is a registered trademark of Penguin Group (USA) Inc.
The "J" design is a trademark belonging to Penguin Group (USA) Inc.

PRINTED IN THE UNITED STATES OF AMERICA

10 9 8 7 6 5 4 3 2 1

1

Agnes Glitch was a fine-looking woman, and she had money, but she was alone in the world. Her father had made a fortune in the gold fields, and then he had died, leaving Agnes's mother a rich widow. Then a few years later, when Agnes was already a grown woman, her mother had died. Agnes was left with a small fortune and no family, living alone in St. Louis. Tonight, she had gone out to the Pink Lady, one of the fanciest nightclubs in the city, and she'd had a couple of drinks, the fancy, colored kind, pink, they were. She was watching the show and enjoying herself a bit, although she was alone. As she stood up to make her way to the hallway that would lead her to the ladies' powder room, she noticed that there were a number of people looking at her. She paid no attention to that—she was used to it. She was a kind of minor celebrity in St. Louis: young, pretty, and rich.

She made her way to the hall. There was no one else in it at that moment. As she was walking down the hall toward the powder room, she came to a room in which two men were arguing. She did not understand any of their words, and she was going to hurry on past, but suddenly one of the men pulled out a pistol and shot the other one. As the unfortunate man fell, the other looked up, smoking gun in hand, and Agnes found herself looking the man straight in the face. She was horrified. She ran the length of the hallway, right past the powder room, to an exit door. She went through the exit door into the night and kept running.

The man with the gun checked the body quickly to make sure that his victim was dead. Then he stood up and ran into the hall. Looking toward the exit door, he saw that the hallway was empty. He ran to the exit door and went outside. He stood for a moment looking around. There was no sign of the woman.

"Damn it," he said. He tucked the gun away underneath his coat and walked around the building, going in the front door. No one noticed him. Already a minor panic had set in. There were people hustling toward the hallway. He could not see over their heads, but it was obvious to him that someone had heard the shot, investigated, and discovered the body. Some people were leaving the nightclub. A tough-looking man in a three-piece suit spotted him and walked over casually to stand beside him.

"Everything all right, Slick?" the man said.

"No," the shooter said.

"What's wrong? Did you get him?"

"I got him all right," said Slick. "He's deader'n a rock. But I was seen."

"Who—"

"That rich gal. Glitch. She was walking down the hallway and looked in the room just as I shot him."

"Maybe she never got a good look. Maybe—"

"She got a good look all right," said Slick. "We looked

at each other right smack in the face. Then she ran. I ran after her, but she had already gone outside. I couldn't see her in the dark. She got away."

"She'll go to the cops, Slick. She'll tell them—"

"We have to get her first. Come on."

They headed for the front door, but before they reached it, a big man in a gray suit stopped them. "What's your hurry, Hannah?" the man said.

Slick turned to face the man. "No hurry," he said. "It's just past my bed time."

"What do you know about that stiff down the hall?"

Slick Hannah looked at his cohort with a surprised expression. "Stiff?" he said. "Ziggie, do you know anything about a stiff?"

"No, Slick. This is the first I heard."

"Chief Johnson here wants to know about a stiff."

Ziggie shrugged. "I can't help him none. Can you?"

"I was kinda wondering what all the commotion was about in here. We just now come in to get a drink, me and Ziggie here, and we wondered what all the excitement was about. So someone found a stiff, did they? Do you know who the stiff was?"

"We know him," said Johnson. "You know him, too. It was Charlie Dode. It ain't no secret that you had a grudge against him."

"Well, now," said Slick. "I wonder who it was done him in for me like that."

"My guess is that it was you—or one of your boys. Maybe Ziggie here pulled the trigger for you."

"Now, see here," Ziggie said.

"Chief," said Slick. "I didn't have no use for Charlie. We was business enemies. Business. That was it. And I had him outsmarted. I didn't have no reason to kill him—or to have him killed. You're looking in the wrong rat hole."

"I think I know what rat I'm looking for," said Johnson. "We'll talk again. Don't leave town."

Johnson turned and walked away. Slick Hannah leaned toward Ziggie and spoke low. "We got to get over to the Glitch house right now," he said.

Agnes Glitch did not go home. Her dress was a little smart, but it would do for everyday. She had enough cash on her to last her for a while. She made her way as quickly as she could to the railroad station and asked for the next train out of town. It was due to leave at any moment, and it was heading west. She bought a ticket and boarded the train. She felt a little relief as it huffed its way out of town, but she was watching through the window to see if anyone had followed her, if anyone suspicious had boarded the train after her. She had not seen anyone. She seemed to have been the last passenger to board, but she was still nervous, still suspicious of every lone man on the train.

Agnes knew who the killer was. Slick Hannah was notorious around St. Louis. She did not know the details. She only knew that he was some kind of a gangster and that the police were always after him. His picture had been in the papers more than once. In fact, she knew that he was the owner of the Pink Lady, the very nightclub she had been in when she had witnessed the murder. Hannah had long arms, and she knew that he would not want to leave a witness to what he had done. He would not want to leave her running loose. If he could figure out where she had gone, he would follow her and kill her.

• • •

Back in St. Louis, Slick and Ziggie arrived at Agnes's house in their buggy and parked the buggy in the street a couple of doors down. Then they got out and walked the rest of the way. The house was dark. The neighborhood seemed to have gone to bed. They made their way around the house to the back door and tried it. It was locked. "Break in," Slick told Ziggie. Ziggie found a rock and smashed a window. They stood quietly for a moment after that to see if the noise had alerted anyone. It seemed not to have. Ziggie crawled through the broken window and went to open the door. He let Slick in, and quietly, the two men went through the entire house, but they found no sign of Agnes.

"She's got a bunch of valuable stuff in here," said Ziggie.

"Forget it," said Slick. "Let's get the hell out of here."

Back at the club, Chief Johnson and his men were still questioning some of the patrons. No one had seen anything. A few had heard the shot, but most said that they had thought nothing of it. A few had been curious. One bold man had gotten up and walked down the hallway to check it out. He had seen the body in the room, but he had seen no one else in the hallway. Then an elderly woman had excitedly stepped forward.

"I saw Agnes Glitch go down the hallway," she said, "and now that I think about it, I never saw her return."

"Agnes Glitch," said one of the cops. "That's that young, rich woman."

"I know who she is," said Johnson. "So she went down the hallway and never came back?"

"That's right," said the woman. "She never returned. I know, because she was sitting right in front of me. She did not come back."

The cop looked at his boss. "Do you think she shot Dode?"

"I think it's much more likely that she saw the shooting and ran for her life," he said.

"Oh, my," said the woman.

Johnson pulled the cop aside. "We have to find Agnes Glitch," he said. "Take a couple of the boys and look for her. Start with her house. If she's not there, check the railroad station and the stage depots. Look everywhere. Get going now."

When the train was well out of St. Louis, Agnes relaxed a little. No one had made a move toward her, and everything seemed all right. She knew, though, that Slick Hannah would soon figure out that she had left town. He would soon figure out that she had taken the train and which train it was. And then he would come after her. She would have to figure out what to do next. Wherever the next stop was, she decided, she would get off the train and catch a stage to somewhere, some out-of-the-way place, some place Hannah would never think of, the least likely place for a woman like her to go.

Then she realized that the police might also be looking for her. She was nearly as well-known around St. Louis as Slick Hannah. Someone in the club had likely seen her go down the hallway, and they would tell the police. She would have Slick Hannah and his gang as well as the police on her trail. She had to think really hard and figure this one out. She wondered how far they were from the first stop.

• • •

Back in St. Louis the cops who had gone looking for Agnes returned to the police station and reported to Chief Johnson.

"She wasn't at home," one of them said. "But someone else had been there. They broke a window in back of the house and got in that way. The back door was standing open."

"So Hannah's after her," said Johnson. "Damn it. We have to find her first."

"We checked all over," said the other cop. "The only possibility we came up with was that there was a train leaving just a few minutes after the killing. The man at the station said that a woman came up in a hurry and bought a ticket. He didn't actually see her board the train, but he assumed that she did—"

"She was well dressed, he said," the other cop broke in, "and she didn't have no luggage."

"That had to be her," said Johnson. "It all fits together. She saw Hannah, recognized him, and he saw her. She ran for her life. Where was the train going?"

"Down into Indian Territory. From there, she can catch something going up into Kansas, and from there, she's got several possibilities."

"Wire the U.S. marshal in Fort Smith, Arkansas," said Johnson. "And wire the chief of the Cherokee Nation. Give them her description and ask them to watch for her. Give them Hannah's description as well and suggest that they detain him if they see him. Get going now."

Ziggie burst into Slick Hannah's office, rushed over to the desk, put both hands on the desk, and leaned toward Slick. "Boss," he said, "she got on a train and headed west."

Slick stood up and went for his hat. "West," he said. "Where west?"

"Indian Territory," said Ziggie. "Seems like she just run into the train station and bought a ticket on the next train out. It headed toward Indian Territory. That's the end of the line. But when she gets there, she can catch any one of a number of trains headed other places. Mostly they all go someplace up in Kansas."

"Gather up the boys," said Slick. "About six of them. Meet me at the station as soon as you can."

"We catching a train?"

"You heard me. Get going."

Ziggie rushed out of the office again. This time Slick was close behind him. When they got outside, they went in two different directions.

Not long after that, Chief Johnson and one of his assistants were in the train station. The assistant tapped the chief on the shoulder. "What is it, Tobe?" said Johnson.

"Look over there, Chief," said Tobe. "Ain't that Hannah buying a train ticket?"

"It damn sure is," said Johnson.

"I thought you told him to stay in town. Want me to arrest him?"

"Leave him alone," the chief said. "He's not running away. He has too much here in St. Louis to run away. He's after the Glitch gal. Keep out of sight. We'll follow him."

2

The train chuffed into Joplin, Missouri, and made an unexpected stop. Agnes was puzzled. She was also worried that someone was after her and might catch up. She stopped a black porter who was walking down the aisle. “Did I hear that we were in Joplin?” she asked.

“Yes, ma’am,” he said.

“How long will we be here?”

“Maybe about an hour.”

“Then we’ll go on in to Indian Territory?”

“Yes, ma’am. Straight into Vinita.”

“Are there other connections here—in Joplin?”

“Yes, ma’am. You can catch a train into Baxter Springs or Lawrence or several other places from here in Joplin.”

“Thank you,” she said. The porter walked on. Agnes waited a moment, then got up and left the train. She went straight to the ticket counter in the station.

“Where’s your next train going?” she asked.

“First stop’ll be Baxter Springs, then on to—”

“How soon does it leave?”

“About twenty minutes.”

"I'd like a ticket, please," she said, digging in her purse.

Johnson and Tobe watched as Slick Hannah, Ziggie, and six other men boarded the train headed for Indian Territory. Then Johnson walked to the counter. He bought two tickets. Then he said, "I'm Chief Johnson."

"I know that," said the ticket agent.

"I don't want to be seen on this trip. Can you get us into the caboose?"

"Follow me," said the agent. He led the way to the caboose and spoke to a brakeman. The man nodded, and Johnson and Tobe were let into the caboose. They had not been seen by the Hannah gang.

In a passenger car, the eight gangsters got settled into their seats. Ziggie said to Slick, "I ain't never been to Indian Territory. What's it like?"

"Hell, I ain't never been there neither. I imagine there'll be a bunch of Indians whooping around."

"They got towns. And they got trains going in."

Hannah made no answer. "They said we was going into a place called Vinita," said Ziggie.

"Likely a bunch of tepees," Slick said. "Maybe a great big one for a station."

"What'll they do when white men come into their town?"

"They might try to take our scalps," Slick said. "How the hell should I know?"

A bald-headed gangster sitting directly across from Ziggie said, "The red bastards better leave my scalp alone."

• • •

"What are we going to do when we get to Vinita?" asked Tobe.

"Try to keep out of sight," said Johnson, "but try to keep the Hannah bunch in our sight. We need to watch and see if they locate Miss Glitch."

"There's eight of them, Boss," said Tobe.

"And two of us. I know. Tobe, we'll have no jurisdiction out there. We'll have to contact the local law and ask for his cooperation. I'm playing this by ear. The main thing is that we need to protect Miss Glitch. Not just for her own good, but we need her for a witness against Hannah."

Agnes got onto her second train in Joplin almost unnoticed. The agent who sold her the ticket knew she was on the train, but no one else seemed to be aware of her presence. This train was not nearly as crowded as was the first one. She settled back, wondering what she would find in Baxter Springs and wondering what she would do when she got there. She dropped off to sleep eventually, and she was startled awake when the train lurched to a stop. She sat up quickly, blinking her eyes and looking around. She could see out the window that they were at a station. She wondered if they could be at Baxter Springs so quickly. Then she saw the sign over the door of the station: BAXTER SPRINGS. She made up her mind quickly. The more she could change directions, the better off she would be. She left the train and went into the station.

"Where do your trains go from here?" she asked.

"This one will take you on to Lawrence," the man said.

"I don't want to go to Lawrence."

"Well, if you wait an hour—"

"I'd rather not. Is there a stagecoach station?"

"Just down the street."

Along the way, Agnes saw a gun shop. She looked in the window for a moment, then walked in. When she came out again, she had a loaded Merwin and Hulbert Company .38-caliber, five-shot pocket pistol in her purse.

John Slocum had just killed a man in Caney, Kansas. The man had started a fight with him and it had wound up in gunplay. Slocum had won. There had been plenty of witnesses, so he had not been charged in the killing. Still, he had killed a man, and he did not like hanging around after such things happened. He had ridden all the way to Coffeyville and through it and was still going. The next town would be Baxter Springs. He had no reason to go to Baxter Springs. He did not know why he was even going east. Even so, he kept riding. Perhaps, he thought, he would turn south from Baxter Springs and ride down into the Cherokee Nation. He wasn't sure. That way would take him on to Texas. He would sure rather be in Texas than in Kansas.

Some people said that Texas was flat, and it was in some places. But it also had hill country, lots of hill country, and it had the beaches way down south. Texas had variety, lots of variety, and Slocum liked that. Kansas had nothing but flat. When the wind picked up, and it almost always did in Kansas, great tumbleweeds blew across one's path, sometimes blew right into one while he was riding along with his head ducked down for protection against the wind. When that happened, it could spook a horse. He'd heard of a few men who had been hurt, a couple even killed, when their horses had been hit by tumbleweeds traveling fast in the wretched Kansas wind. Yeah, he made up his mind. He would go on to Baxter Springs, get a good meal, maybe get drunk, maybe lay up for the night with a cozy little whore, get up in the morning, have breakfast, and then turn south. He would ride through Indian Territory and on down into Texas. By the time he got there, he'd be needing a job. There were plenty of big ranches in North Texas.

The stagecoach was traveling from Baxter Springs toward Coffeyville, and to Agnes, the ride was awful. The coach bounced frightfully, now and then almost throwing her across and into the man sitting opposite her. He was a great, fat, sweaty man with a red face, who breathed heavily all the time as if he had just climbed a steep hill. To the fat man's right sat an elderly lady, prissy as hell. To his left, a preacher, holding his Bible in his lap, his eyes constantly looking up as if into the sky, but, of course, they could not see any sky while riding in the coach. Agnes figured the man must be constantly praying, perhaps for a smoother ride. From time to time, she thought about asking him to pray for her, but she wouldn't have wanted to tell him why.

Agnes herself was seated in the middle of the other seat with a whiskey drummer on her right and a man on her left who appeared to her to be a gambler. The whiskey drummer was a small man, mild-mannered and quiet. The gambler, if such he was, was another story altogether. He kept trying to drag Agnes into conversation, kept asking her questions that were none of his business. He wanted to know where she was from and where she was going. She dodged his questions, but that made him the more persistent. He said that his name was Calvin Black. She kept hers to herself.

Suddenly there were loud voices outside, and the coach jerked and lurched to a quick stop. The gambler stuck his head out the window for a look, but a shot sounded. He brought it back in.

"You have a box up there?" someone said.

Inside the coach, they could hear the sound of the heavy strongbox being dragged, then dropped with a dull *thud* to the road. "Now toss your guns down," said the same voice. They heard the guns hit the road. "Climb down." In another moment both the driver and the shotgun rider had apparently gotten down, for the man behind the voice rode to the door and bent to look in. He opened the door. "Everyone out," he said. "You men, keep your hands held high." The passengers came out of the coach one at a time, and the bandit leader had them line up in a straight line along with the driver and shotgun rider. Then he climbed down off his horse. Four other bandits still sat on their horses holding guns. All of them were masked.

The leader put his gun away and opened up a sack. He started walking down the line. Neither the driver nor the shotgun rider had any cash, neither did they carry watches. The next in line was the elderly lady, who opened up her purse, but the bandit leader said, "We don't rob ladies, ma'am."

He moved on to the preacher, who said, "I'm a man of the cloth."

"I don't give a damn, Preacher," the bandit said. "Empty your pockets."

"This is outrageous," the preacher said, tucking his Bible under one arm and digging into his pockets. He deposited cash and a pocket watch in the sack. The outlaw pointed the muzzle of his six-gun at a medal that was hanging around the preacher's neck.

"I'll have that," he said.

"It'll do you no good," said the preacher.

"I'll have it anyway."

The preacher grumbled as he pulled the chain on which the medal was hanging over his head and dropped the medal and chain into the sack.

"Thanks, Preacher," said the bandit.

"I'll pray for your soul," the preacher said.

"Suit yourself." He stepped in front of the fat man who huffed and puffed and poured all his wealth into the sack, never saying a word. Next came Agnes. The bandit stopped and studied her for a moment, then stepped on down the line. Agnes thought of all the money she was carrying, and she thought about the loaded pistol in her purse, but the bandit did not rob ladies. Her heart was pounding, nevertheless, as the bandit stepped in front of the whiskey drummer. He took the case of samples and everything else the poor man had. The gambler was last.

"I'll see you hang for this," the gambler said.

"If you do," said the bandit, "I hope you enjoy the spectacle. Right now, empty your pockets. You can start with that gun you got underneath your coat."

The gambler carefully took out a pocket pistol and dropped it into the sack. Then he emptied his pockets of money and a watch. The bandit poked at a diamond stickpin in the gambler's necktie, and the gambler unfastened it and dropped it into the booty sack. Then a ring. The bandit then picked up the guns the driver and shotgun rider had dropped in the road. He handed the sack and the guns to another of the gang, and then he heaved up the box from where it had landed in the road and passed it up to another rider. At last he mounted his horse again, looked at the lineup of his victims, touched the brim of his hat, and said, "Thank you all very much. It was a pleasure meeting up with you." Then he turned his horse and kicked it in the sides. "Let's go, boys," he called out, and the gang rode off in a cloud of dust. Just then, Slocum came riding down the road.

The gambler stepped out and waved his arms. "Hey there," he called out. "We've just been robbed. They went that way. If you hurry, you can catch them."

Slocum rode on up to the stage and stopped.

"Well, go on," said the gambler. "They're getting away."

"How many of them?" asked Slocum.

"Four or five," said the gambler. "Hurry."

"There were six," said the driver. "All armed, and they took all of our guns."

"Pretty heavy odds, don't you think?" said Slocum. "Why don't you just ride on in to Coffeyville and report it to the sheriff?"

"They'll get away," said Calvin Black, "and they've got all of our money and our guns."

"They don't have all of our money," said the elderly lady. "They don't rob ladies."

"They robbed me," said the preacher, "a man of the cloth."

"Well," said Slocum, "you ain't no lady."

Agnes tried to drown a smirk, and although Slocum noticed it, he didn't say anything. He did notice her good looks though.

"So you're not going to do anything?" said Black.

"I don't see how me riding alone after six bandits and getting myself killed would do any of you any good," said Slocum. "Tell you what I will do though. Since you're all unarmed, I'll ride along with you to Coffeyville. Just in case."

"That's mighty thoughtful of you, stranger," said the driver.

"Yes, it is," said Agnes, "Mr.—"

"The name's Slocum."

"Mr. Slocum," she said, and she looked at Black, "I'm sure we all thank you."

The driver and the shotgun rider climbed back onto the seat, the passengers all crawled back into the coach, and Slocum turned his big Appaloosa around. With a lurch, the coach started moving again.

3

The six bandits rode up to a lone line shack several miles north of the road on which the stagecoach had been robbed. They put their horses into a small corral behind the shack and unsaddled them. One man stayed behind to feed the horses while the other five went into the shack. One man carried the sack, another carried the strongbox, and a third carried the extra guns. Inside the shack, the men tossed their ill-gotten gains onto a table. One man went to put on some coffee to boil. All of the men had pulled down their masks. They were young, clean shaven, and had the look of carefree cowboys. In another couple of minutes the man who had stayed behind with the horses came walking in.

"Bartley," said the man who had done the talking during the robbery, "dump that sack out on the table."

The man called Bartley lifted the sack by its two bottom corners and turned it upside down, dumping the contents out. The "boss" started separating the cash from the other stuff. "See if you can get that box opened," he said. Bartley and another man began working on the lock to the box.

"Say, Aubrey," said one of the cowboys, "if we ain't

gonna keep this stuff, how come we're bothering to count it?"

"Curiosity," Aubrey said. "And it looks like a pretty good haul. Now put it back in the sack." He turned toward the two men working on the box. "How you doing there?"

The lock snapped, and Bartley opened the lid and shoved the box toward Aubrey. "See for yourself," he said.

Aubrey went through the contents of the box. He found one letter, or rather an envelope, bearing the inscription, *Sheriff Clive Thornton.* He put everything else back and opened the envelope. There was a stack of bills, but no note or name indicating who the money was from. He handed the money to Bartley and said, "Here. Count it out and divide it up."

Slocum rode into Coffeyville with the stagecoach. The sun was already low in the western sky. He decided to put off his trip to the Indian Territory and on down into Texas until tomorrow. It would be dark soon, and it was too late to go riding a strange trail. He left the Appaloosa standing at the hitch rail and helped the two ladies out of the coach while the driver and the shotgun rider were busy getting the luggage off the top of the stage and out of the boot in the rear. Agnes walked into the station to make some inquiries of the agent. Slocum noticed that she had no luggage. Agnes stepped aside, apparently trying to make up her mind about something. Calvin Black stomped into the station and started complaining loudly about the robbery. The fat man and the drummer were waiting their turns. Slocum decided that there was no need for him to hang around. He turned to walk away, but he felt a soft hand on his shoulder. He looked, and there was Agnes.

"Excuse me," she said.

Slocum took off his hat.

"Yes, ma'am," he said. "What can I do for you?"

"May I talk to you in private?"

Pulling into Vinita, Indian Territory, the train blew its whistle long and loud. Men and women stood beside the track just watching. Children came running and dogs started barking. Some horses reared, frightened out of their wits, and men fought to control them. At last it came to a stop. From the caboose, Johnson and Tobe watched out the window as Slick Hannah and his gang disembarked. They stood looking around at the crowd for a short spell. The crowd and the town did not look that much different from other frontier towns of the day. The only difference was that some of the people were obviously Indians. They were dressed like everyone else though.

"Wait here," said Slick, and he walked alone into the station. There was a crowd at the counter. Slick shoved his way through. "Hey," someone said, but Slick ignored it. At the counter, he looked at the agent.

"Wait your turn, mister," the agent said.

"I'm in a hurry," said Slick. "Just answer me a question. On the last train from St. Louis, did you see a pretty young woman get off? She'd a been traveling alone without no bags."

"No," said the agent. "I saw no one like that, but then, I wasn't on duty."

"Who was?"

"Carey Tomlinson."

"Where can I find him?"

The agent wrote down an address and shoved it toward Slick who picked it up and read it to make sure he could read the man's writing. Then he turned and left the station. Outside, he handed the paper to Ziggie and said, "Find out where this is." Ziggie took the paper and walked away to question people in the crowd. In a few minutes, Ziggie returned.

"I know where it's at, Boss," he said.

"Lead the way."

They walked down the street, turned a corner, and walked two more blocks to a small frame house. Slick took the paper away from Ziggie and studied it. Then he studied the house. "Come on, Ziggie," he said. "The rest of you wait here." Slick and Ziggie walked to the front door, leaving the others standing in the street. Slick pounded on the door. No one answered. He pounded again.

"If it was me," said Ziggie, "I wouldn't be sitting around in a dump like this on my day off."

Slick looked at Ziggie. "You're right," he said. "Let's check the saloons around town."

It did not take long before they discovered that there were no saloons. Liquor was illegal in Indian Territory. "So what the hell does a man do on his day off?" said Slick.

"Sit around and jack off?" said Ziggie.

"If he was doing that," said Slick, "he'd a been at home."

Down the street, two men hurried into the sheriff's office. Sheriff Fourkiller was seated behind his desk. He looked up to see the two men. "Hey," he said, "what are you two so excited about?"

"We was just down at the railroad depot, Eddie," said one of the men.

"Yeah," said the other. "A city dude that had got off the train came in and shoved his way through the crowd."

"Real tough acting," said the other.

"Yeah. He asked about a woman he was looking for."

"Came in on the last train."

"Billy said he wasn't working. Gave him Tomlinson's address."

"Then the tough guy leaves the building and meets up with some others and they go off together."

"Hold on just a minute," said Fourkiller, leafing through some papers on his desk. He found the telegraph he had received from the chief repeating the information from the police in St. Louis. A woman and a city gangster. It could be. He stood up. "You two are deputized," he said. "We'll pick up some more men on the way. How many of them were there altogether?"

"I think there was eight of them," said one of the men, and they followed Fourkiller out the door.

From the caboose, Johnson and Tobe had watched as the Hannah gang left the area of the station. They got off the train and walked out, following the gang, trying to hold back and keep out of sight. They had watched as Hannah and Ziggie had knocked on the door of the house and then left disappointed. The gang had stood around not far from the house talking, when a man had come walking down the street carrying something in a bag. They watched as he walked up to the very house Hannah and Ziggie had approached.

As the man unlocked the door and opened it, Slick said to his boys, "Stay here," and he ran up to the door, stopping the man before he could get inside. "Hey," he said, "is your name Tomlinson?"

"Yes," said the man, looking nervously from Slick to the other men out on the street. "What do you want?"

"I'm looking for a woman who came in on the last train from St. Louis. Not the one just now but the one before that. The guy at the station told me you was on duty. That right?"

"Yes. I was."

"This gal would have been alone, and she didn't have no bags. Well?"

"I didn't see anyone like that," said Tomlinson.

"Listen, wise guy," said Slick, "I know she got on the train at St. Louis and I know it was headed here. How could you miss a gal like that?"

"Maybe she never came here," Tomlinson said. "The train stops at Baxter Springs, Kansas. She might have got off there. She could have caught any one of a number of trains going different places in Kansas and even on to San Francisco."

"You sure you never seen her?"

"I never saw anyone answering that description."

"Damn," said Slick, turning to hurry back to his gang.

Back down the street, Johnson and Tobe stood in the shadows of a grove of trees. "I wonder what that was all about," said Tobe.

"Slick sure doesn't seem to be happy with whatever he found out," said Johnson.

The gang started back in the direction they had come. Johnson and Tobe watched them go. They had just about disappeared from the policemen's view before Johnson stepped out of the shadows to follow them. He stopped so abruptly that Tobe ran into his back. There were five men approaching. The one in front was wearing a badge. Fourkiller and his hastily thrown together posse had come around the other side of the block and missed the Hannah gang completely. They spotted Johnson and Tobe however.

"What are you men doing here?" Fourkiller demanded.

"You look to be the local law," said Johnson.

"I'm Sheriff Fourkiller, and I been told to be on the watch for men like you."

"I think you were warned about the same men I'm following," said Johnson. He reached for his inside coat pocket, hesitated, and said, "May I?"

"Go ahead," said Fourkiller.

Johnson drew out his wallet and badge and showed it to Fourkiller.

"I'm chief of police in St. Louis," he said. "A young woman witnessed a murder there recently. We believe the killer saw her at the same time. Somehow she got away from him. She's running for her life, and he's following her, we believe, to do her in before we can find her and get her to testify."

"So you followed them here," said Fourkiller.

"That's right. They left the station and came over here. Hannah, that's the ringleader, talked to a man in that house there." He pointed to Tomlinson's house.

"That's Carey Tomlinson's place," said a member of the posse.

"Let's go over there and see what they talked about," Fourkiller said.

Tomlinson saw them coming and stepped out into the yard to meet them. "Hello, Sheriff," he said, looking not at Fourkiller, but at Johnson and Tobe.

"Carey," said Fourkiller, "did you just talk with some city folks?"

"Just one. I seen the others waiting for him over there."

"What did you talk about?"

"He asked me if I seen a woman alone get off the train from St. Louis without baggage."

"Did you?"

"No. And I told him I'd remember something like that. That made him mad. He said he knowed that she got on the train in St. Louis, so I told him that it stops in Baxter Springs, and she mighta got off there. That was it. He left."

Fourkiller looked at Johnson. "So what do you do now?" he asked.

"Keep following him. Hope I can find her before he does. I don't have anything to arrest him on yet. I need that girl. She's the only witness."

"Is there any way we can help you?"

"No way that I can see. Thank you anyway."

"Well, boys," said Fourkiller, "it looks like you're all dismissed. Thank you. Chief, sorry I couldn't be any more help to you, but I wish you good luck."

"Thank you, Sheriff," said Johnson.

4

Agnes Glitch had about had it. She had taken one train out of St. Louis, caught a second train, and then boarded a stagecoach, which had been robbed. Of course, she had been spared, but who knows what would happen if it occurred again? Now she was in Coffeyville, Kansas, with no idea of where to go next. She could take the next train or the next stage and not worry about its destination, but there were bound to be limits as to how long she would be able to keep that up. She was beginning to want a change of clothes. She wanted a bath. She wanted a good meal. She had plenty of money on her—for now. But that would run out one of these days, and then what? She could go to a bank and have them contact her bank, but then she would be giving away her location. She had not thought of any of this stuff when she had left St. Louis. She had thought only about the face of that Slick Hannah, looking into her eyes, holding that smoking gun. She had run.

Slocum had solved one of her problems. He had taken her to a nice restaurant and found them a table in a far corner of the room. It was private. They ordered a good meal.

She had a glass of wine. Slocum had ordered whiskey. He behaved like a perfect gentleman, although she had never before kept company with a gentleman who dressed like he did. She guessed that he was a cowboy out of work, or worse, a gunfighter. She had heard of gunfighters. She wondered if he wanted a job. She could pay him. She did not want to face what she had to face all alone.

"Slocum," she said. "I'm glad that you happened along out there today."

"Oh," he said. "I didn't do anything."

"You've been good company to me when I needed it."

"Well, I'm glad I could do that," he said. He had a feeling that she wanted to tell him something more, but he didn't press her about it. He did not want to pry. Instead he poured them each a fresh drink. She picked up her glass and sipped her wine.

"Slocum," she said, "I—"

She hesitated.

"What is it?" he said. She had given him an opening. She had not given her name. "Are you in some kind of trouble?"

"I hardly know you," she said. "But I have to talk to someone. For some reason, I feel like I can trust you."

"I can keep my mouth shut," he said.

"My name is Agnes Glitch."

Slocum did not respond. It had been a statement and did not call for a response. She waited nevertheless to see if he registered any surprise or any interest. He did not.

"You haven't heard it before?"

"Should I have?"

"Then the news hasn't reached out here," she said.

"That's good. I think the St. Louis police may be looking for me."

"Is that where you're from?" he said. "St. Louis?"

"Yes."

"And why would the police be looking for a lady like you?"

"I saw a murder. I was the only witness."

"And how do the police know that you saw it happen?"

"I don't know that they do, but I'm well-known in St. Louis. I'm afraid that someone saw me go down the hallway and told the police." She went on to describe the whole scene. Slocum thought about it for a moment.

"I can see how they could be looking for you," he said. "But why don't you want to tell them what you saw?"

"The killer was Slick Hannah. He's a notorious gangster in St. Louis. If I tell the police what I saw, he'll have me killed before I can testify in court. Slocum, there's more."

"Go on then."

"Hannah is almost certainly after me."

"So if you've got it figured right, this Hannah character is after you to kill you, and the police are after you because you're their only witness."

"That's right."

"I noticed you're traveling light. You must've left St. Looie in a big hurry."

"I ran out of that club and went straight to the train station. I didn't look back except to watch over my shoulder for anyone who might be following me."

"You want to just keep on running for the rest of your life?"

"No. I don't. But I don't know what else to do."

"I have an idea," Slocum said. "Why don't we talk about it some more in the morning. Why don't we go shopping for some new clothes for you? And then why don't we go over to the hotel and get you a room and a bath? You can get a good night's sleep. You'll feel better in the morning."

"I have to keep moving, Slocum. Hannah could show up any time. I—"

"I'll watch over you. Don't worry. I'll be right outside your room all night."

"You'd do that?"

When he'd heard about the stagecoach robbery, Sheriff Clive Thornton of Coffeyville had put together a posse and he had been riding the countryside the rest of that day. When night fell, the sheriff and his posse stopped to make a camp until daylight. Thornton was determined to catch the robbers. No one knew, but he had a special package in that strongbox. It was the payoff for a particularly sleazy job he had done for one of the big local ranchers. He wanted it, and he meant to have it. He had told the posse as soon as they got out of Coffeyville that if they spotted the robbers they were to shoot to kill. No one questioned his orders. It would save the expense of a trial.

They were all beat from a long day of riding, and they lounged around the campfire, either sipping coffee or whiskey. Thornton had his own bottle, which he shared with no one, drinking right out of the bottle. Thornton was pretty sure who the robbers were. Any ordinary road agent would have taken everything. They had taken only from the men, leaving the ladies alone, and they had taken the strongbox. It had to be that goddamned Aubrey Newman and his brothers and cousins. They were the ones Thornton had helped old John Crowe, the big rancher, bilk out of their property. They were trying to make Thornton look bad, and it was already working. People in town had been talking about how he wasn't doing his job with bad men running loose around the countryside robbing the stage and so on. Well, he would get them. Kill them all.

Aubrey Newman and his partners had ridden into town, slipping in the back way under cover of darkness. They stopped back behind the stagecoach depot, hidden well back in a grove of trees, and dismounted. Aubrey had already prepared a note, which he had deposited in the sack with the stolen goods and money. The note read, *Here is all the stuff I tuck from those good folks. See that they get it back. And here is the cash box. Everything is here. Even the guns.* He looked at his brother Bartley.

"Go on over there," he said, "and open that back door. Be careful."

"I'll get it," Bartley said. Ducking low, Bartley ran the distance to the depot's back door. He fooled around for a spell, then he turned and ran back to the others. "It's open," he said.

"Give me that stuff," said Aubrey, and one of the others handed it to him. Aubrey ran, and when he reached the depot, he went inside. Looking around quickly, he deposited the stuff on the big desk against the back wall. Then he stepped back out and shut the door. He ran back to where the others waited for him. They all mounted up and rode away out of town.

Agnes savored the hot bath. New clothes were hanging up in the room, she'd had a good meal and a few glasses of wine, and she felt safe with Slocum sitting in a chair in the hallway just outside of her door. It was the best she had felt since leaving St. Louis. She was having certain thoughts about Slocum, this man she hardly knew. He was a kind man, she thought, a gentleman, and he was pretty good-looking. She fantasized about inviting him in to spend the night with her in her room. She imagined it, but she could not bring herself to do anything about it. She could only fantasize.

Johnson and Tobe had to hide until the Hannah gang was once more on board the train. Then they had managed to get into the caboose again. The train was headed back for Baxter Springs. Tobe was smoking a cigar and Johnson was puffing his pipe. "I wish we could just arrest the bastards," Tobe said.

"They'd just get out again," said Johnson. "We have to have Agnes Glitch. With her, we'll put Hannah away for good. We might even get him hanged."

"I'll get me a front-row seat to that one," Tobe said.

"You can sit right beside me," Johnson added.

"What do you think will happen next?"

"They'll get off at Baxter Springs and ask if anyone saw Miss Glitch get off the train there."

"And if anyone remembers her and where she went, they'll follow her again," Tobe said.

"That's about it," said Johnson.

In the passenger car, several of the Hannah gang were dozing, but Slick was sitting up with a determined look on his face. Ziggie was nodding and woke up with a start as the car gave a lurch. He looked at Slick, sitting there wide awake.

"Slick," he said.

"Yeah? What?"

"Slick, how come we got to chase this broad all over the Wild West? She's run away scared to death. She knows what'll happen to her if she ever shows her face back in St. Louis. She ain't going to talk. Why can't we just forget her and go on back to the city?"

"Listen, dummy," Slick said. "She saw me do the deed. Yeah, she's running right now, but what happens when she gets tired of running? Huh? When she runs out of dough? All her bank accounts are back there. She'll have to come back. And if we quit looking for her, the cops won't. They know she's the only witness. If we don't get to her first, they'll find her. One of these days, they'll find her, and they'll bring her back. And there ain't no statute of limitations on murder."

Slocum sat in the hallway smoking a cigar. He was wide awake. A few people came down the hall and went into their rooms. He had not seen anyone suspicious looking. He thought about Agnes Glitch, a fine-looking woman, but a woman in trouble. He did not blame her for running. What if she had gone to the cops with her story? Would they have been able to protect her from these gangsters? He doubted it. What cops, what all the lawmen in the country, were good for—if anything at all—was catching someone after he had done the deed. So the way it would likely have played out was that the cops would have promised her protection, the gang would have killed her, and the cops would have arrested the murderer—maybe. Yeah. Running was a good choice for a woman alone in that situation.

But what should she do now? He had told her they

would talk about it again in the morning. It seemed he had dealt himself in on this deal. So he had to think of something. He had to have something to tell her in the morning. Maybe she would think of something herself, but he really hoped that she would relax and get a good rest. She sure did need it. Well, he would buy her a breakfast in the morning, and then they would talk. He'd come up with something.

Aubrey Newman and his boys were riding back toward the line shack when they saw the campfire. Aubrey halted them. "Who might it be?" said Bartley.

"It could be a posse," Aubrey said.

"I bet it is," said Bartley.

"Let's get in real close and take a good look."

They dismounted and led their horses for a distance, then they walked on without the horses. Close enough for a good look, they could see that it was a group of men. The horses were all tied. The men were all asleep. One man snorted and rolled over, his face toward the small fire. Aubrey recognized him in the firelight.

"It's Thornton all right," he whispered. "Cut those horses loose and drive them off. Burl, go back and get our horses. Lead them up here. The rest of you, get your guns ready in case they wake up."

Burl went for the horses while Bartley went to cut loose the posse's mounts. Aubrey and the rest stood ready with their guns. Burl brought the horses down, and Bartley had the others all cut loose. Aubrey joined him, and they gathered up the reins of all the horses. They led them away quietly. Then they mounted up and, still leading the posse's horses, rode away fast, yelling and firing their weapons.

Back at the campsite, Thornton and the others came out of their sleep. "What the hell?" shouted Thornton. But no one made a move. The horses and the horse thieves were already out of sight in the darkness.

5

Slocum and Agnes were having breakfast in one of the nicer places in town. They did not talk about Agnes's troubles while they ate nor while they had an extra cup of coffee. When they were finished, the other customers had all left the place. It was safe to talk.

"What we have to do," Slocum said, "is try to keep you out of sight."

"We're not doing a very good job of that just now, are we?" Agnes said.

"I think we're okay. Even if they manage to track you, it will take them some time. You were smart making those changes along the way. But we ought to do something pretty soon."

"I think I should just go farther west," Agnes said.

"You'll just be running your whole life," said Slocum. "What we need to do is solve this problem."

Just then, the door opened and a nice-looking woman who looked to be in her late forties walked in and stepped over to the counter. A little bell over the door had tinkled as the door opened and shut, and the woman who ran the eatery stepped out of the back room. A smile spread across her face. "Hi, Maudie," she said.

"Hello, Jeanne," said Maudie. "Have you got one of your delicious apple pies left?"

"I sure do. It was just cooked this morning."

"I'd love to have it," Maudie said.

Slocum sat up and looked over his shoulder. There was something familiar about the voice.

"I'm thinking I should get back to the room," said Agnes. "Not be seen out in public so much."

"Excuse me a minute," said Slocum. He stood up and walked toward Maudie. Her back was turned to him.

"Maudie?" he said. "Maudie Newman?"

Maudie turned, and pleasant surprise lit her face.

"John Slocum," she said. "Well, I'll be danged." She threw her arms around Slocum and hugged him tight to her bosom. Slocum hugged her in return. "What brings you here?" she said.

"I was just passing through," he said, "but something's come up. Are you living around here?"

"We got a little spread just out of town," she said. "How've you been?"

"Let's talk about that later, Maudie. Is Hiram with you, and the boys?"

"We're all still together."

"Maudie, I have someone I want you to meet. Right over here."

Jeanne brought out the apple pie, and Maudie said, "Hold on a minute, John." She paid Jeanne for the pie and took it with her to the table where Agnes was sitting.

"Maudie," said Slocum, "this is Agnes. She's a new friend of mine." Maudie gave Slocum a knowing look, and he added, "It's not what you're thinking. Agnes, this is Maudie Newman, an old friend. Maudie, would you sit down for a minute?"

He pulled out a chair for her, and Maudie sat down. Slocum resumed his own seat. "Maudie," he said, "Agnes is in some trouble. I'll fill you in on it later. Right now, she needs a place to hide out. Do you think you might have some room at your place?"

Maudie looked from Slocum to Agnes and thought for only a few seconds. "Sure," she said. "We can manage. When do you want to come out?"

"The sooner the better," Slocum said.

"I've done all my shopping," said Maudie. "This pie was the last thing I had to do. If you're ready, we can go out together right now."

"We just have to run over to the hotel and get Agnes's clothes," Slocum said.

"My buggy's just outside."

Soon Agnes and Maudie were riding in the buggy with Slocum riding alongside on his Appaloosa. As they moved along, Slocum filled Maudie in on all the details of Agnes's dilemma.

"Well, Agnes," Maudie said, "don't you worry about a thing. John will take care of your troubles, and in the meantime, you can stay with us out at the ranch. It won't be no bother, so don't fret none about it."

"That's very kind of you," said Agnes. The urge she had to head west was gone, and the idea of hiding out on a ranch outside of Coffeyville, Kansas, was appealing—under the circumstances. And she had confidence in Slocum somehow, even though she had just met him. He had stood guard over her all night and had not made a move toward her. He was a gentleman. But a part of her wished that he had made a move. Well, there was still time for that. And Maudie seemed as nice as she could be. When this was all over, she thought, she would pay Maudie well for her help, Slocum too. She could certainly afford it.

Out on the lonesome prairie, Sheriff Thornton and his posse were sorefooting it along toward the nearest ranch, which was a good five-mile walk from where their horses had been driven off. A few of the men had hangovers from the night before, and all were dirty and sweaty and stinking. There was much grumbling and considerable cursing going on.

"God damn it, Clive," said one of the men limping along, "you sure got us in a hell of a mess this time."

"Aw, shut up, Shorty," said Thornton. "How could I know that someone would run our horses off like that?"

"You could've posted a guard last night."

"Yeah."

"Who?" said Thornton. "You was all drunk as skunks. Who coulda stayed awake to watch? Just tell me that."

"If you'd a assigned someone, you could'a made him stay sober."

"If you don't all shut up," Thornton said, "I'll arrest the whole goddamned bunch of you and throw your asses in jail when we get back to town."

"On what charge?"

"Interfering with an ongoing investigation."

"Bullshit."

When the train stopped in Baxter Springs, the Hannah gang all got off, and Slick went immediately into the station to inquire about Agnes Glitch. The agent had a vague recollection.

"There's just been too many people through here since then," he said.

"Well, think hard," said Slick. He pulled a fifty-dollar bill out of his pocket and held it up for the man to look at. The agent's eyes got big. "I need to find that woman. How many women travel through here alone and without luggage?"

"It's coming back to me," the agent said. "Yeah. Yeah, I kinda recall now. I told her the next train would take her to Lawrence, and she said she didn't want to go to Lawrence. I told her a stage would be leaving for Coffeyville right away, and the last I seen of her, she was headed toward the stage depot. I can't swear to you that she took the stage, but I never seen her again."

Johnson and Tobe watched through the windows of the caboose as Slick Hannah rounded up his gang and headed off down the street.

"Where the hell could they be going?" said Tobe.

"You think you could follow them and find out?" said Johnson.

"I think so."

"Without being seen?"

"Yeah. I can do that."

Tobe left the car and crept along the street behind the gang. After a couple of blocks, Slick went inside the stage depot. Tobe lurked against a building on the other side of the street. In a few minutes, a stagecoach came rolling up and lurched to a stop. A man came out of the office and busied himself changing the horses. Four passengers got off the stage, collected their luggage, and went off in different directions. When the stage was ready to go, the entire Hannah gang came out of the depot and crowded into the stage. Soon it was rolling its way out of town. Tobe hurried across the street and went into the depot.

"Can I help you?" said the man behind the counter.

"Tell me about that bunch that just left on the stagecoach," Tobe said. He flashed his badge. The man was impressed. He didn't bother asking anything about jurisdiction.

"They came in and wanted tickets for the stage headed west," he said. "I told them it already had a couple of passengers and there wasn't room for all of them. He asked who the passengers were, and I told him. They was sitting right over there. Well, he went and bought them off. Paid them pretty well for their tickets too."

"Where are they going?"

"Caney," said the man.

Tobe hurried back to the train to tell Johnson.

Agnes had gotten settled into an extra bedroom at the Newman ranch, and Maudie was busy preparing the noon meal. Slocum was sitting in the living room with a cup of coffee visiting with Hiram Newman, Maudie's husband and an old friend of Slocum. Agnes came out of the bedroom and went into the kitchen, offering her assistance to Maudie. Of course, Maudie refused, instead giving Agnes a cup of coffee and suggesting that she go into the living room and relax. The sound of several horses riding up to the house carried through the walls, and Slocum gave Hiram an inquiring look.

"That'll be the boys," Hiram said.

In another moment the door opened and six young men

came walking into the room. Aubrey Newman was in front. He stopped and looked at Slocum, astonished.

"By God," he said. "Is that Slocum?"

Slocum stood up.

"It's him all right," said Hiram.

Aubrey rushed over to shake hands with Slocum and pat him on the back.

"It's been a long time, Aubrey," Slocum said.

"Too long, I'd say," said Aubrey. "Do you remember my little brother?"

"I don't remember him that big," said Slocum. "Is it Bartley?"

Bartley grinned and shook hands with Slocum. "I sure do remember you," he said.

Aubrey pointed to the other men in his group. "This here is my cousin Finis, and this is his brother, George. These other two boys work for us. Joseph and Isaac Croy."

Slocum shook hands all around. Aubrey was looking with curiosity at Agnes, who was also looking at him. Slocum noticed the glances they were exchanging. "Boys," he said, "I want to introduce you to Miss Agnes Glitch. She's a guest here in your mama's house, Aubrey."

Sheriff Thornton and his posse rode into town past noon. They all looked as if they had been run over by a train. They were riding horses they had commandeered at the first ranch they had come to. Two of the men were actually crying from pain and exhaustion. Thornton's face was puffy and red. They all went straight to the nearest saloon. Thornton had just sat down with a beer when a man from the stage depot came running in. He ran straight to Thornton.

"What the hell is it?" Thornton said. "No, we didn't catch the bastards yet."

"I seen you ride in," the man said. "What I come to tell you is that all the loot from the robbery was returned last night."

"What?"

"Yessir. Someone broke into the office and left it on the desk. The watches and guns they took. The money they took off the passengers. The lockbox. Everything."

Thornton was thinking about his own money, but he wanted to be careful what he said.

"Was there, uh, a letter for me?" he asked.

"Why, no, Sheriff. Should there a been?"

"Oh, it ain't nothing," Thornton said. "It'll likely come along later."

"Why the hell would anyone rob the stage and then bring back all the goods?" said Shorty.

"Must be crazy," said another member of the posse.

"Yeah," said Thornton. "They're crazy all right."

6

"What the hell are we going to do?" Tobe said.

"Let's get something to eat and think about it," Johnson said, his brow was wrinkled. He was obviously already thinking about it. They walked down the street until they found a place, then they went inside and ordered meals. While they were waiting, they drank coffee.

"The next stage out won't be until tomorrow morning," Tobe said.

"We can't wait that long," said Johnson. "That would put them a day ahead of us, and if they're on the right trail, they might find the Glitch woman before we catch up to them."

"Yeah," Tobe said.

A waiter brought their meals, and they ate in silence. When they were finished, they had one more cup of coffee.

"I wonder if the train goes on," said Johnson. "We can check the train schedule."

"It's already left," Tobe said.

"There might be another one," said Johnson.

"In this rube town?" said Tobe. "I doubt it."

"Well, let's check anyhow."

They paid and left the eatery. Then they walked back to the train depot and checked with the agent. There was not another train going west for some time. They went out to the sidewalk where Johnson lit a cigar. They stood there in silence for some minutes, Johnson looking up and down the street. Suddenly his eyes lit on a sign down a ways that read: LIVERY. He tossed aside the stub of his cigar and said, "Come on."

Night was falling, and Slocum had gone out to sit on the porch and smoke a cigar and sip some good brown whiskey. Aubrey and the rest of the boys had gone to the bunkhouse for the night. Maudie was still puttering about in the kitchen and Hiram had gone to bed. Slocum heard the door opening and he turned to see Agnes coming out on the porch. He stood up.

"Do you mind some company?" she asked.

"Of course not," he said.

She sat down in the chair next to his, and Slocum resumed his seat.

"What are you thinking about?" she asked.

"Nothing much," he said. "Just relaxing."

"I guess that's good," she said. "I can't do it. I keep thinking about Slick Hannah and his gang."

"They ain't totally out of my mind," Slocum said, "but there's nothing I can do 'til they show up. When that time comes, I'll figure what to do."

"You're an amazing man," Agnes said. "Not many men would hang around to face a strange woman's problems for her."

"A woman alone in this world needs some help sometimes. No real man would run away and leave her to face trouble by herself. Besides," he smiled and looked at her, "you ain't so strange."

Agnes laughed, and Slocum did too. "You are," said Agnes. "You're a strange one indeed."

"I've been called a whole lot worse than that."

"Should I call you John? Maudie calls you John."

"Slocum'll do just fine. I never have been able to break Maudie of that habit of calling me John."

"All right, Slocum."

"You haven't called me anything but 'ma'am.' I wish you'd call me Agnes."

"All right, Agnes."

"Slocum?"

"Yes?"

"I know these are your friends. I should call them my friends too. They're being very kind to me."

"Is something wrong?"

"It's Aubrey. I've seen him before. And I think all the other boys who were with him."

"Oh yeah? Where?"

"There were six men who robbed the stagecoach. I know that Aubrey was the leader. He recognized me too. I could tell it."

"I thought I saw something kind of flash between you two."

"Yes. Well, that was it."

"You say there were six of them?"

"Six."

"The other five must have been the five with him now."

"I think so."

"There must be some pretty good explanation," said Slocum.

"I hope so."

"Well, let me worry about that. I know they're not dangerous. I mean, there's no danger to you."

"No. I didn't think so. I just thought that you ought to know."

"Thanks for tipping me off."

"Slocum?"

"What?"

"You know where my bedroom is?"

"I know."

"Why don't you slip in tonight?"

"You don't have to do that, Agnes. I ain't insisting—"

"I know you're not, and I know I don't have to. I want to. If you don't—"

"I don't know about trying to slip through the house at night."

"I'll leave the window open on the back wall."

Calvin Black was having a drink at the bar of his own saloon in Coffeyville. He had seen Agnes Glitch walk away with Slocum, and he couldn't get her out of his mind. He wanted that woman, wanted her bad. And he already did not like Slocum because of his refusal to chase after the stage robbers. It did not matter that his gun and money and watch had all been returned to him. He could not have known that would happen, and neither could Slocum have known. He had not seen Slocum or Glitch since they had walked away from the stage depot. While he was thus engaged in thought, a man walked up to him.

"Calvin," he said.

Black looked at the man. "Yeah? What is it?"

"I just thought you ought to know there's a preacher out front preaching in the street. He's drove away several of your customers with his hoorawing."

"Is that right?" said Black. He downed the rest of his drink and headed for the door. He stood for a moment looking out over the batwings. It was the preacher from the stage standing in a wagon bed and haranguing a small crowd of men who had gathered around. He had not realized that his own crowd had been so noisy until then. They had drowned out the preacher's voice inside the saloon. Angrily, Black went outside and pushed his way through the crowd to stand just by the wagon bed.

"Right inside that saloon," the preacher was saying, "men are pouring the devil out of a bottle and into their mouths to sink down into their stomachs and let his evil out into their bodies. They're paying good money to pave the road to hell, to smooth their own ride down into that inferno. They're—"

"Preacher!" Black shouted.

The preacher stopped and looked down at Black.

"Why, you were one of my fellow passengers on the stagecoach," he said.

"I want you to shut up, Preacher," Black said. "You're driving business away from me."

"What is your business?"

"That saloon right there is my business, and you're keeping customers out."

"I'm sorry to hear that, friend, but if that saloon is your business, you're in the wrong business. It's an affront to the Lord. It's—"

"God is God and business is business," said Black, "and if you go on trying to spoil my business, I'll have to drag you off that wagon."

"The work of the Lord cannot be stopped by violence."

"We'll see if it can."

Several members of the crowd began to laugh.

"My friends," the preacher shouted, "this wicked man—"

Black grabbed hold of one of the preacher's pant legs and pulled, and the preacher fell over backward in the wagon, screaming. The crowd roared with laughter. Black dragged the preacher howling out of the wagon, and dropped him hard on his back in the dirt. All the wind was knocked out of the preacher's lungs, and he lay there gasping for breath.

"Come on inside, boys," Black shouted. "The drinks're on me."

The whole crowd followed Black inside the saloon. The preacher lay squirming and gasping. Eventually he managed to get some air into his lungs. He sucked hard, and finally he sat up. He got hold of the side of the wagon and pulled himself to his feet. Picking up the Bible he had dropped, he pulled himself up straight and tall and stalked his way through the batwing doors. He held the Bible up high over his head and shouted, "Oh, you sinners."

Black glanced at his bartender and said, "Get a couple of the boys and drag that son of a bitch out of here."

The preacher was in the middle of the saloon roaring out a condemnation when the three men grabbed him and pulled him out the front door. The crowd inside the saloon laughed loudly and continued drinking and playing cards and fondling the women who were sitting on their laps. Black heaved a sigh of relief and went to a nearby table to sit.

• • •

Slocum found his way quietly around the house. Everyone had gone to bed, and the place was quiet. He found the open window and slipped through it silently.

"Agnes?" he whispered.

"I'm here," she said.

Slocum's eyes adjusted to the dim light in the room, and he saw her sitting on the bed. She was not wearing anything, and even though he knew that she was a good-looking woman, the sight of her like that took his breath away. He reached down to pull off his boots and place them quietly on the floor by the window, and then he made his way over to the bed. He was starting to pull off his shirt, and Agnes got out of the bed to help him with it. Soon she had him as naked as she was, and she pulled him to her and kissed him hard.

Breaking loose at last, she crawled back into the bed, pulling him behind her. She lay back and spread her legs, and Slocum crawled on top of her, between her long and lovely legs. He leaned forward to kiss her again, and his hands found her breasts, and he took one in each of his hands, caressing and kneading them. Her hands traveled down to his throbbing cock and his sack of balls and fondled them, stroking the already hard tool.

She guided the head of his rod into the wet slit of her cunt, and he drove down, plunging the entire length of the tool into the dark, damp, depths of her cavern. "Oh yes," she whispered. "Give it to me. Give it all to me." He thrust up and down, in and out, and her upward thrusts matched his. "Ahh," she sighed. "Ahh, yes."

Back in Coffeyville, in an alley behind the saloon, fists pounded the preacher, who was bruised and bloody. His face was cut and a few of his ribs were broken. He could hardly stand, could not have stood, but one of the men held him up from behind. Two others took turns bashing fists into his face and into his stomach. At last one of the men stepped back. The other kept hitting the preacher.

"That's enough," said the one who had stopped.

The other hit the preacher with a roundhouse right that must have broken the jaw. The preacher's head dropped to his chest, and the man standing behind him let go and allowed him to drop to the ground. One of the other men knelt beside him and went through his pockets for all the money he could find. He pocketed the money, noticed the medal around the preacher's neck, jerked it loose, and dropped it in a pocket, and then all three men ran out of the alley. The preacher did not move.

Slocum was awake early, well before daylight. He sat up carefully because Agnes was still in a deep sleep and he did not want to awaken her. She needed that sleep. He stood up and carefully put on his clothes, then crept across the room to pull on his boots. He gave her one last look. She had not moved. He slipped out the window and walked back to his room.

Someone walked into Clive Thornton's office in Coffeyville. Thornton looked up from behind his desk.

"Clive," the man said. "We just found a dead preacher in the alley behind the saloon."

7

Slocum rode into town that morning to have a look around, mainly to see if any city folks had come into town. None of them, not the police nor the gangsters, had ever seen him. They would not suspect him of being involved in any way. He arrived just as Sheriff Clive Thornton was walking into the alley behind the saloon, followed by a small crowd of the curious. Slocum casually took note of that fact as he tied his Appaloosa to a hitch rail outside the saloon, which was not yet open. He stood on the sidewalk for a bit looking up and down the street and then decided to get some breakfast. He walked back to the same eatery where he'd had a meal with Agnes and went inside. He took a table and looked around at the people who were in there, who all appeared to be local folks. He ordered his meal and drank coffee while he waited for it to arrive. Then he ate and had another cup of coffee. He paid for the meal and left the place.

When he walked outside, he saw the stagecoach come into town. At the depot, eight men in city clothes came out of the coach. They looked mighty relieved to be getting out of the crowded contraption. One of the men stepped out from the crowd and stood looking around the town. Slocum sauntered down toward them.

"Another dump," one of the men said.

"Go inside and ask about the woman," Slick said to Ziggie. Ziggie went inside, and Slocum walked on by casually. He crossed the street and walked back to the saloon. This time he found it open and went inside. The barkeep, who was wiping the bar down, looked up at Slocum and asked, "Can I help you?"

"You have coffee on?"

"Sure."

"It's a bit early for anything else," Slocum said. "At least for me."

The barkeep poured him a cup, and Slocum paid for it. He stayed at the bar.

"It looked like there was some excitement going on out there this morning," he said.

"Somebody beat a preacher to death last night out in the alley," said the barkeep.

"A preacher, huh?"

"Yeah. He was out in the street driving off our business. The boss went out and stopped him, but he came in here later. Me and a couple of the boys dragged him out. Never saw him again."

Just then Clive Thornton came walking in. He stopped at the bar just beside Slocum and gave him a look. "Who're you?" he asked.

"Name's Slocum."

"What're you doing in Coffeyville?"

"Riding through."

"Was you in town last night?"

"Nope."

Thornton looked at the barkeep. "You ever seen him before?"

"Nope. He wasn't in here last night—or anytime else 'til just now."

"So, Ernie, what happened to the preacher in here last night?"

"I was just telling this fellow about it," the barkeep said. "After Calvin went outside to shut the man up, he come in here and started in. Me and two other boys dragged him out and threw him down in the street. We came back in and I never seen him again."

"That was it?"

"That's it."

"God damn it," said Thornton. "It looks bad for a town when a preacher gets killed."

"He was a troublemaker," said Ernie.

"Even so, it looks bad. Did anyone go out of here right after you left him in the street?"

"I didn't see anyone go out."

Ziggie came out of the depot and walked over to Slick Hannah. "She came in here all right," he said. "The man remembers her. He didn't see where she went though."

"She didn't leave again on the next stage?"

"Nope. The man said that a fellow named Calvin Black what owns the saloon down the street was awful interested in her though."

"Come on," said Slick. The other seven men followed him to the saloon. They all walked inside and up to the bar. "You Calvin Black?" Slick asked Ernie.

"That's my boss," Ernie said.

"You're strangers in town," said Thornton.

"You're very observant," said Slick, looking at Thornton's badge. "And you got a strange little town here."

"We like it. What brings you men to town?"

"How come you asking about Calvin Black?"

"He's an old friend."

"He usually comes in later," said Ernie. "Maybe another hour or so he'll be in."

"We'll wait," said Slick.

"I could sure use a drink," said Ziggie.

The other men agreed with him eagerly. Slick said, "Give us a round."

"What'll it be?"

"Whiskey. Straight up."

Ernie poured them a round, and Slick paid for the bottle and kept it. The gang all moved to a table, leaving Slocum and Thornton standing at the bar. Ziggie leaned across the table to speak low in Slick's ear.

"I don't like having that hick lawman in here," he said.

"He's no problem," said Slick.

"Well, I don't like it."

At the bar, Ernie said to Thornton, "You have any luck tracking down those weird stage robbers?"

"Not yet," said Thornton, "but I'll get the bastards."

"Real strange," said Ernie, "them robbing the stage like that and then returning all the loot."

"Yeah," said Thornton. "It's real strange all right." He was thinking about his lost money. Apparently no one else knew that it had been in the box. The robbery had been only to get his money. The criminals had to be those goddamned Newmans, but Thornton had to get the proof. Either that or he had to just catch them alone and kill them one at a time. That wouldn't get him his money back though.

Slocum finished his coffee and said, "Well, I got to be going." He walked out of the saloon and headed for his horse. He had all the information he could get out of town for the time being. He knew that the gang from St. Louis was in town, and he knew that the sheriff had not made any progress in tracking down the stage robbers. He mounted his big Appaloosa and headed for the ranch.

Out on the road leading to Coffeyville, a buggy bounced along. It was being driven by Police Chief Johnson. Tobe was sitting uncomfortably next to him, holding his hat on his head with one hand, and doing his best to keep from being bounced clear out of the buggy.

"Chief," he said, "do we have to go so fast?"

"We don't want Hannah and his boys to be too far ahead of us," said Johnson.

"I don't believe this buggy was meant to be drove like this. It was meant for driving slow on smooth roads."

"We'll make it all right," said Johnson.

"My butt will be ruined," Tobe said.

"You'll survive."

The buggy hit a rut and gave a hard bounce that nearly threw Tobe out. Johnson left the seat for an instant and came back down hard. The bowler on his head fell off, but it landed on the seat between the two men.

"Damn it," Johnson shouted.

"Oh, hell," said Tobe.

Johnson slowed the horse and pulled the buggy to the side of the road and stopped. He picked up the bowler and put it back on his head. "We'll take a short break," he said.

"Another bump like that," said Tobe, "and we might loosen a wheel. Might break it. Might break an axle even. Then we'd be stuck out here on this damn lonesome road. What would we do then? Unhitch that horse and both of us climb on its back without even a saddle?"

Johnson climbed down slowly out of the buggy and stretched. Tobe followed. He stood rubbing his sore ass.

"Knock off the bellyaching," Johnson said. "I don't like this Wild West any more than you do, but we've got a job to do, and I mean to see that we do it."

"All right," said Tobe. "All right."

"When we find Miss Glitch," said Johnson, "we accomplish two things. First of all, we save her life. In the second place, we get us a witness to a killing that Slick Hannah either did himself or had done. We've never been able to get a witness against Hannah before. Remember those two things, Tobe. When you start feeling sorry for yourself, remember them."

"Yes, sir," said Tobe.

"You ready to get going again?"

"Yes, sir."

They climbed back into the buggy, and Johnson started driving again. This time, however, he went a little more slowly.

Calvin Black walked into his saloon. He was surprised to see eight men looking like city dudes sitting at a table and drinking whiskey. He was surprised to see anyone drinking whiskey that early in the day, and he was surprised to see these strangers in city duds.

"Morning, boss," said Ernie. "Coffee?"

"Sure," said Black. He was looking at the strangers.

"Morning, gents," he said. "What brings you fellows to town?"

"You Calvin Black?" said Slick.

"That's right." Ernie put a cup of coffee on the bar.

Black picked it up and took a sip. "Anything I can do for you?"

"I want to talk to you," said Slick. "Come on over and have a seat."

Black walked to the table, taking his coffee with him. Slick turned in his chair and reached over for a chair from the next table. He dragged it up for Black to sit on. Black sat down. He looked at Slick with curiosity.

"I'm looking for someone," Slick said.

"I'll help if I can," said Black.

"A woman."

"Well, most of the girls are still asleep. They work late, you know, but I—"

"Not that kind of a woman," said Slick. "I'm looking for a woman who came in here from St. Louis."

"Oh," said Black. He thought immediately of the woman from the stage. She had a city look. And she had been traveling light, traveling without any luggage, a strange thing for anyone, especially a city lady, to be doing. It became obvious to Black all of a sudden that the woman had been running from these men. He wondered why.

"May I ask why you're looking for this woman?" he said.

Ziggie leaned forward with a snarl on his face. "If you seen her," he said, "you better talk up."

"Take it easy, Ziggie," said Slick. "She's an old friend. There was a misunderstanding. I need to talk to her. That's all."

"Well, I, uh, I may have seen her."

8

While Slick Hannah was quizzing Calvin Black, Johnson and Tobe rolled into town in the buggy. The first building they spotted was right at the edge of town. It was a livery. Johnson pulled in there and left the buggy and the horse in the care of the liveryman. He and Tobe walked to the door and stood there looking out.

"What now?" Tobe asked.

"We need to find out if Hannah and his gang are here," said Johnson. "But in case they are here, we need to do it without letting them spot us."

"How are we going to do that?" asked Tobe.

"Take off your hat and your jacket," said Johnson.

"What?"

"You heard me. Do it." He held out his hands. Tobe took off his hat and handed it to his boss. Then he shrugged out of his jacket and did the same. Johnson studied him for a moment. "All right," he said. "Get that tie and collar off." Tobe was left standing in his shirt sleeves, collarless and hatless. "That's better," said Johnson. "As far as we know, Hannah doesn't know you. And now you don't look quite as much like a city man as you did before. I want you to go find a store and buy some clothes. Make yourself look like you belong here. Dress like a farmer or a cowhand or something. Once you've done that, get us a hotel room. Then come back here for me."

Slick Hannah and Ziggie had gone into Calvin Black's office with him to talk more privately. Slick had moved behind the big desk and seated himself in Black's chair. Black was left with nothing to do but take a chair across from Slick. Ziggie stood nearby.

"Tell me about the woman," said Slick.

"I only said I might have seen her," Black responded.

"Tell me about the one you seen."

"She was well dressed, a little overdressed, I'd say, and she was traveling alone and without any luggage. She got off the stage here."

"Is she still around?"

"What, uh, what is this information worth to you?" said Black.

Slick looked at Ziggie, and Ziggie smacked Black across the face. Black's face showed astonishment more than pain. His eyes were wide.

"It might be worth something to you," Ziggie said. "It might mean you don't get all your fingers broke."

"Now, wait a minute," said Black. "You can't come into my own place of business and do that to me. The sheriff here is a good friend of mine. You can't—"

Ziggie stepped behind Black and jerked the chair out from under him. Black sprawled on the floor, and Ziggie stepped on his left hand. With his free leg, he kicked Black in the ribs. Slick stood up and leaned with both hands on the desk so he could look over and see Black there on the floor.

"Don't bother yelling for help," he said. "My boys are all out there. They'll stop anyone from coming in here to help you." Ziggie kicked Black again. "Now," said Slick. "Tell me what I want to know."

"All right. All right," said Black. "I never saw her leave town."

"Help the man back into his chair, Ziggie," said Slick.

Ziggie leaned over, catching Black by his coat lapels. He dragged him to his feet. Then he picked up the chair and sat Black down hard in it. He patted Black on the cheeks.

"Is that better?" he said.

Black looked at Ziggie in disbelief.

"So?" said Slick.

"So—what?" said Black.

"If she never left town, then where is she?"

"I don't know," said Black. Ziggie raised a hand, and Black continued as fast as he could talk. "She left the depot with that cowboy. I think he called himself Slocum. He rides an Appaloosa."

"What the hell is an Appaloosa?" said Ziggie.

"It's a big horse with a spotted ass."

"Hey," said Ziggie, "I seen one like that when we come into town."

"Yeah," said Slick. "Me too. I remember it."

"That's the last I ever saw of her," said Black. "I swear it."

"So where does this Slocum hang out?" said Slick.

"I don't know that. He's a stranger in town. The first time I ever saw him was out on the road. I was coming back to town in the stage. The woman was on the stage too. We were held up by a gang of outlaws. That Slocum came riding up, but they were already gone. He was too late to do anything about it. He rode along with us 'til we got into town though. Right after that, the woman walked off with him. That's all I know."

"Okay. Okay," said Slick. "So we got to find that cowboy with the spotty-ass horse. You're going to help us too."

"I will," said Black.

"You fix meals here?" said Slick.

"I can take care of it for you."

"Good. You got any rooms in this joint?"

"I have a few upstairs."

"Fix us up with some food and some rooms. We'll stay here."

Aubrey and his boys were out riding the range. Aubrey and Bartley had separated from the rest, who were rounding up cattle. Aubrey and Bartley had ridden to the far eastern edge of the range. What was beyond was water and the land that Thornton had helped John Crowe steal from the Newmans. While they sat at the newly erected fence staring across at what had been their land, some Crowe cowhands came riding up. They stopped at the fence just opposite Aubrey and Bartley.

"Howdy, boys," said one of the Crowe hands. "You all doing all right today?"

"We'll make it," said Aubrey.

"You seem to be studying this land over here," said the cowhand. "It's fine grazing land, ain't it?"

"It's mine," said Aubrey.

"Now, I wouldn't be talking like that if I was you," said

the other cowhand. "It's talk like that what leads to range wars and such."

"Gets people killed," said his companion.

"You never know who might get killed when something like that comes along," said Aubrey.

"You ain't threatening us, are you?"

"Just making an observation. That's all."

"Well, I'd be mighty cautious if I was you." The two Crowe cowhands turned their horses and rode off laughing. Bartley's hand went for his six-gun, but Aubrey saw it and reached out with a hand to hold his brother's wrist.

"Be patient, brother," he said. "It ain't the right time."

"I'd sure like to shut up their laughing."

"Later," said Aubrey. "You go find the other boys. I'll see you back at the house after a while."

Bartley turned his horse and rode off, leaving Aubrey to sit and stare at the lost land.

When Tobe returned to the livery, it was all Johnson could do to keep from falling over on the ground and rolling with laughter. He did not fall over, but he did laugh. When he at last stopped laughing and was wiping the tears away from his eyes with his pocket handkerchief, Tobe, a grumbling expression on his face, said, "What's so damned funny?"

He was standing there in his new overalls, brogan shoes, and flannel shirt, with a straw hat on his head. His old clothes were in a bundle under his arm. There was a slight bulge under the left side of the bib of his overalls, and Johnson knew that was where Tobe had stashed his gun.

"Never mind," said Johnson. "You look just fine. Did you get us a room?"

Tobe pulled a key out of his pocket and held it out to Johnson. "I've got another," he said.

"Good." Johnson pocketed the key.

"I walked past the saloon on my way back," Tobe said. "They're in there. Hannah and his gang."

"Can I get to the hotel room without being seen?"

"I think so. They're all busy feeding their faces. But there's a back door to the hotel. If you hurry across the street and go around to the alley, you can get in the hotel without much of anyone spotting you."

Slocum made it back to the ranch. After Maudie had greeted him and given him a cup of coffee, he got Agnes to go out on the porch with him. They sat on chairs out there, and Slocum sipped his coffee. Then he said, "I think that city gang is in town."

"Slick Hannah?" she said.

"Well, of course, I never seen them before," he said. "But there was eight city fellows that come into the saloon while I was in there."

"Eight of them," she said. "It has to be the Hannah gang."

"One of them asked the barkeep about a man named Calvin Black, the owner of the place."

"Black was on the stage with me," said Agnes. "He'd remember me all right."

"Then likely they'll know you're somewhere around here," said Slocum.

"Oh God," she said. "I have to get away from here."

"No, you don't," said Slocum. "You're safer just sitting here. You've got all the protection you need."

"I don't know," she said. "Maybe you're right. Oh, Slocum, I just don't know what's the right thing to do."

"Then leave it to me," he said. "No one knows where you are. You're safe."

Maudie stepped out onto the porch just then. "Are you two having a nice conversation?" she said.

"Yes, Maudie, we sure are," said Slocum. "By the way, where's your biggest boy?"

"Aubrey?" she said. "He rode out this morning with the rest of the boys to round up some cattle. They ought to be getting back pretty soon. They'll all be as hungry as a bunch of hogs."

Thornton had ridden out to the John Crowe ranch and was sitting with old man Crowe in his parlor. They both had a glass of whiskey in their hands.

"I've got that piece of range fenced off now," Crowe was saying. "It's working out real well. I don't have nearly so far to drive my cows to get them a good drink."

"I'm glad you're happy with the results," said Thornton. "Now I need to get paid for what I done for you."

"What are you talking about?" Crowe said.

"I ain't been paid. That's what I'm talking about."

"I told my banker in Baxter Springs to send you the cash money on the stage," Crowe said. "He assured me that he would do it. You should have got it already."

"What stage was it on?" said Thornton. "The one that got robbed the other day?"

"Well, I don't know about that," said Crowe. "I guess it coulda been."

"'Til it gets into my hands," said Thornton, "it's still your money. If it was on the stage that was robbed, it was you that got robbed, not me. You still owe me."

"Wait a minute. Let's talk about this."

"You still owe me, god damn it."

"All right. Don't get your bowels in an uproar. I'll pay you. I'll have to send one of the boys to the bank for the money. I don't keep that much cash around the house here. Have you tried to catch the robbers?"

"Of course, I've tried."

"No luck, huh?"

"Not so far," said Thornton. "But I'm pretty sure I know who the bastards are."

"Who is it you suspect?"

"The Newmans, of course. Especially that oldest boy, that Aubrey."

"Why don't you arrest him?"

"I got no proof. The only thing like proof would be if I told them about the money you sent me. I don't want to do that, and I don't think you want me to."

"No. No. Of course not. Well, I'll send Hobbs for the cash."

Johnson and Tobe took turns looking out their hotel window at the front door of the saloon across the street. Night had fallen when they saw a young cowboy ride into town. They had no way of knowing that the young man was Aubrey Newman or that the woman they were looking for was safely ensconced at Aubrey Newman's ranch not far out of town.

9

Aubrey had not told anyone that he was going to town. He had sent his brother away to work with the other hands, and he had sat and stared at his lost land for a while. The more he thought about it, the worse he felt. It had been some satisfaction stealing Thornton's money and making a fool of the sheriff in the doing of it, but it had not gotten his land back for him. He still had his share of the cash in his pockets, and the longer he sat and thought, the more he decided that he needed a drink. Maybe a couple of drinks. It wouldn't hurt anything if he should run into that damnable Sheriff Clive Thornton either. It would be fun to buy a few drinks with Thornton's money if Thornton was standing by and watching him drink. He turned his horse and headed for town.

By the time he got there, it was dark. He rode right up to the saloon and tied his horse to the rail. He walked inside. The saloon was crowded, and one table was occupied by a bunch of city slickers. He took casual note of them and walked up to the bar.

"Whiskey, Ernie," he said.

Ernie poured him a drink, and Aubrey paid for it. He downed it in one gulp and said, "Hit me again."

Ernie poured another. Aubrey paid again. This time he sipped the drink. He looked around for the sheriff, but Thornton was nowhere to be seen. It was only a minute before Silly Sally, one of the young saloon girls, came walking over to stand by his side. She put a hand on his shoulder and smiled up into his face.

"Hi, Aubrey," she said.

"Hi, yourself, Silly Sally," Aubrey said.

"Buy me a drink?"

"Ernie," Aubrey called out. "Pour another one here."

The whiskey had already gotten to Aubrey's head, and he was feeling like having a wild night. He downed the rest of his second drink and had Ernie pour him a third. Then he paid for both drinks, his and Silly Sally's.

"You want to find a table?" she said.

"Sure thing," said Aubrey. "Wait a minute." He called out to Ernie again, and this time he paid for the rest of the bottle. Then taking the bottle and his glass, he let Silly Sally, carrying her glass, lead him to a table in the back of the room.

Calvin Black walked into the room, and Slick Hannah called him over to the table where he sat with his gang. Black walked to the table.

"Pull up a chair," said Slick.

Black pulled a chair from a nearby table and sat down.

"What've you found out?" said Slick.

"Nothing yet," said Black, "but I've got the boys looking. If they're still around somewhere nearby, the boys'll find them."

"They'd better find them," said Slick, "and pretty damn soon. I'm already sick of this fucking one-horse town."

"An Appaloosa horse like the one Slocum rides is rare around these parts," Black said. "If he's still around, they'll spot him."

Thornton walked in and took a casual look around. He did not notice Aubrey sitting at the back of the room with Silly Sally, perhaps because Silly Sally was draped all over Aubrey, making him hard to detect. He did see the city gang, and he saw Calvin Black. He stepped up to the bar, and Ernie came over to serve him. Thornton noticed a silver medal hanging around Ernie's neck.

"Something new?" he said.

"What?" said Ernie.

"That thing around your neck," said Thornton. "I ain't seen you wearing that before."

"Oh," said Ernie. "Yeah. I've had it a long time. I just never wore it before. That's all. What'll you have?"

"Give me a beer, Ernie."

Ernie brought Thornton the beer, and the sheriff took it and walked over to the table where Black was still sitting with the city slickers. He thought that Black looked sort of like a captive. He grabbed a chair from a nearby table and pulled it up beside Black, causing the gangster who was sitting next to Black to have to scoot his chair to one side. The man did so with a scowl on his face. Ziggie gave a look to Slick. Slick just smiled.

"How you doing tonight, Sheriff?" he said.

"I ain't doing too bad," Thornton said. "What are you boys doing hanging around town?"

"We kind of like it here," Slick said. "You got a nice little town here. We figured we needed a vacation, you know?"

"Yeah," said Thornton.

"You had a busy night here?" said Slick. "Throwing drunks in the calaboose?"

Thornton noticed the jibe, but he chose to ignore it. "Things have been pretty quiet around tonight," he said.

"Yeah. I guess so," said Slick.

Black, greatly relieved that Thornton had come around, pushed back his chair. "Well," he said, "I have some business to take care of, so if you gentlemen will excuse me—"

He stood up and hurried away. "He's a busy man, ain't he?" said Slick.

"I guess he is," Thornton said.

"Say, Sheriff," said Slick, "did you notice that there Appaloosa horse in the street yesterday?"

"Yeah. I seen it."

"You don't know who it belongs to, do you?"

"Sure," said Thornton. "It's that cowboy that was in here when I met you fellows. He calls himself Slocum, I think. Why?"

Ziggie sat up straight. "You mean—"

Slick slapped him on the shoulder. "Shut up, Ziggie," he said. "I'm talking." He looked back at the sheriff. "No real reason," he said. "I just thought he might want to sell him. I'd give him a good price. You don't know where I could find him, do you?"

Thornton shook his head. "He told me he was just passing through." He shoved back his chair and stood up. "Well, I'll see you boys around."

Ziggie leaned in to talk to Slick. "We had the son of a bitch right where we wanted him," he said. "That cowboy."

"Slocum," said Slick. "His name is Slocum, and he's got the Glitch woman."

Black had walked up to the bar. Ernie came over to see him. "You want something, boss?" he said.

"Give me a shot," Black said.

Ernie poured the shot, but before he could turn away, Black stopped him. He reached out and took hold of the medal that was hanging around Ernie's neck. "Where'd you get this?" he said.

"I don't know, boss. I've had it a long time."

"Come here," said Black, dragging Ernie to a corner of the room away from any customers. "You got that off the preacher," he said. "The dead preacher. I seen it around his neck. God damn you, take it off."

Ernie fumbled with the chain and finally got the thing removed from around his neck. "Give me that," said Black, snatching the medal and chain away from Ernie. He dropped it in a coat pocket and said, "Now get back to work."

"You're a big boy," said Silly Sally. "You can take that bottle and me and both of our glasses up to a room anytime you feel like it. I'll show you a time like you never even dreamed of. What do you say, big boy?"

"I ain't quite ready to go upstairs," said Aubrey. "Let's just have another drink right now."

He poured both glasses full.

"What do you want to stay down here for?" said Silly Sally. "There's too many people down here. If you go upstairs with me, I'll take all my clothes off. You can see my whole naked body. You can touch me anywhere you like and do anything else you feel like doing. Come on."

Aubrey lurched to his feet. "Well, all right then," he said. "Let's go."

As Silly Sally got to her feet, Aubrey stood waiting and wobbling. Aubrey leaned forward to grab the bottle by its neck, and he nearly fell over on the table. With Silly Sally's help, he managed to straighten himself up again. Then Silly Sally picked up the two glasses.

"Put your arm around my shoulders," she said.

Aubrey did that, and they started making their way through the crowded room toward the stairway. Silly Sally staggered under the weight of Aubrey on her shoulders as his body kept trying to weave this way or that. As they went by the table where the Hannah gang was sitting, Aubrey bounced against Slick Hannah. He straightened himself up again with a major effort.

"Sorry," he said.

Slick looked up to see a harmless drunk cowboy and a saloon girl. "It ain't no problem," he said.

Silly Sally and Aubrey staggered on. At last they reached the stairway and started climbing, and it was like climbing a mountain. With each step, Aubrey was searching for a foothold, and Silly Sally was pulling hard on the handrail to get them up. Step by step, they went up the stairs. Once Aubrey fell backward and nearly pulled Silly Sally with him, but she managed to keep her balance and keep him upright at the same time. This was no mean feat for Silly Sally, who still held a nearly full glass of whiskey in each hand. At last they reached the landing.

"Just a little ways down the hall," she said. Holding him up, she guided him to a door a short way down the hall, opened the door, went inside with Aubrey, shut the door, put the two glasses down on a table near the door, latched the door, and practically carried Aubrey to the bed. There she dropped him, catching the bottle he still held just before he would have let it fall.

She started to undress slowly, but Aubrey was staring at the ceiling. She finished undressing quickly with no show. Then she went to the bed and crawled in beside Aubrey, whose legs were dangling off the side of the bed. She bent over to kiss him on the lips. He responded—sort of. Then she started getting his shirt off. It was a royal struggle, but eventually, she had him naked. He seemed not to have moved. His legs were still dangling off the side.

Silly Sally got down off the bed and heaved at his legs. In another couple of minutes, she had him lying properly, or nearly so, in bed. Aubrey grinned a foolish grin and reached for her, pulling her down on his chest and kissing her. Silly Sally thought to herself, This is going to be a hell of a chore, but I did ask for it. She had not realized until he stood up from the table downstairs just how drunk he was. But she would make the most of it.

She reached down to his crotch to fondle what she found there, and she was amazed that the tool grew in her hand and developed into a hard rod, ready for action. Aubrey, though, above the waist, did not seem to want to move. She stroked the tool a bit, and he moaned and groaned with pleasure.

"There's more than one way to skin a cat," she said, and she slithered down his body until she had the stiff rod staring at her right between the eyes. She stroked it another time or two, then she put out her tongue and licked it. Aubrey moaned again when, at last, she slurped the entire thing into her mouth. Aubrey gasped with surprise and pleasure. Silly Sally began pumping her head up and down, sucking and slobbering, her drool running down its length to dampen the pubic hairs below.

Aubrey's next groan had more life in it than the previous ones, and he suddenly thrust his pelvis upward, shooting load after load of hot stuff into Silly Sally's mouth. She slurped and swallowed until he lay still again, until he had spent himself thoroughly. Silly Sally pulled her head back and looked at the cock. She stroked it one more time, holding it tightly, until one more drop of the jism came oozing out, and then she licked it up.

Amazingly, Aubrey seemed to sober up and come back to life. She had revived him, and he was like Lazarus risen from the dead. He pulled her to him and hugged and kissed her, and then he rolled her over onto her back and crawled on top of her. Between her legs he found her waiting, juicy pussy and drove his still-hard cock into it and pumped away madly.

Having taken care of whatever business it was he thought that he had to take care of, Sheriff Clive Thornton returned to the saloon. He stopped at the bar and Ernie came over to see what he wanted. Just then, Thornton saw Aubrey Newman and Silly Sally walking down the stairs. "Nothing, Ernie," he said. Ernie shrugged and walked away as Thornton moved toward the stairway. When as Aubrey and Silly Sally got to the bottom of the stairs, they found themselves looking into the stern face of Clive Thornton. Thornton pulled the gun out of his holster and pointed it at Aubrey.

"You get on out of the way, Silly Sally," he said.

Aubrey looked at the gun and slipped his arm from around the shoulders of Silly Sally and said, "Go on, honey."

Silly Sally headed for parts unknown.

"What's this all about, Sheriff?" said Aubrey.

"You're coming with me down to the jailhouse," said Thornton, reaching with his left hand for Aubrey's six-gun.

10

When Aubrey had not returned home by morning, everyone at the Newman ranch was worried. Bartley was quizzed, being the last person known to have seen Aubrey, and he told them that Aubrey had sent him to join the other cowhands. When he left, Bartley reported, Aubrey was still sitting by the fence staring across at the lost Newman land.

"Finis," said Hiram Newman, "you and your brother ride over the range and see what you can find."

"Yes, sir," said Finis, and he left the house with his brother George.

"Joe, I want you and Isaac to ride with me over to the Crowe place. I'll have a talk with the old man."

"All right," said Joe Croy.

"What about me, Pa?" said Bartley.

"Check in town," said Hiram. "Maybe Slocum will go with you."

"I sure will," said Slocum.

Over on the Crowe ranch, old man Crowe had just given Hobbs a packet of money for Sheriff Clive Thornton. "Be sure you hand it to him direct," Crowe said. "I don't want no mistakes about it."

"Yes, sir," said Hobbs. "I'll do that."

"Get going now."

Hobbs had mounted up and headed for town. Along the way, he met Hiram Newman with the Croy brothers. Newman and the two cowhands stopped, effectively blocking Hobbs's way.

"I need to get by here," Hobbs said.

"Can't you stop for a friendly greeting along the way?" said Hiram.

"I didn't think there was nothing friendly between the Crowe ranch and the Newman ranch," Hobbs said. "I'm just minding my own business."

"Say howdy," Hiram said.

"Howdy, then," said Hobbs.

"That's better. Say, I'm on my way to pay a visit to your boss. You reckon I'll find him at home?"

"He was home when I left."

"Thank you. I'll ask you one more question. Have you seen my boy Aubrey anywheres?"

"No. I ain't seen Aubrey for some time."

Isaac Croy was looking at a curious package that was protruding from Hobbs's jacket pocket. It looked remarkably like the packet they had taken from the stagecoach. The one addressed to Sheriff Clive Thornton.

Hiram urged his horse to one side. "We'll be on our way then," he said. "Good day to you."

Hobbs nudged his mount and hurried through the three riders to get on his way to town. Isaac turned in the saddle and watched him go. Hiram had already started riding and

Joe was moving along with him. Isaac said, "I'll catch up with you two in a minute."

"Where you going?" Hiram demanded.

"I'll be right back," Isaac said, and he turned his horse off the road and into the brush. Hiram looked at Joe.

"What the hell's he up to?" he asked.

Joe shrugged. "Damned if I know," he said. "He's just my brother is all."

The two rode on toward the Crowe ranch. Isaac, well off the road, moved quickly. He rode hard and fast until he was sure that he had gotten ahead of Hobbs. He came to a place where there was a ledge beside the road, and he stopped there, leaving his horse well back and out of sight. Pulling his bandana up over his face, he took his lariat and moved to the ledge overhanging the road. In a few minutes, Hobbs came riding along. Isaac waited until just the right moment, then swung his loop. It was a good toss, if not especially great for a cowpuncher, catching Hobbs around the shoulders, pinning his arms and dragging him out of the saddle. Hobbs landed hard on his back, sending up a cloud of dust and knocking the wind out of his sails.

As soon as Hobbs had been jerked from the saddle, Isaac started sliding down the side of the ledge. He was in the road in no time, and he rushed to Hobbs's side, picking up the hat that had fallen from Hobbs's head and cramming it over the fallen cowhand's face. Then he stuck the muzzle of his Colt into Hobbs's ear and thumbed back the hammer. The feel of the cold steel in his ear and the sound of the hammer being cocked were both unmistakable to Hobbs.

"Be still," said Isaac, purposefully grumbling so as to

disguise his voice. Hobbs had little choice but to obey—he had not yet gotten any wind back in his lungs. He lay still, sucking hard for breath. Isaac pulled the package out of Hobbs's pocket and looked at it. On the outside was written, "Sheriff Clive Thornton." Isaac stuffed it into his own pocket and ran back up the side of the ledge as fast as he could go. He mounted his horse and rode off after Hiram and Joe equally fast. He stopped along the way long enough to lift a flat rock beside the road and tuck the package underneath it, and then rushed to get back to the others.

Hiram and Joe were almost to the Crowe gate when Isaac came riding up beside them.

"Where you been?" said Hiram.

"I'll tell you later," said Isaac. "Let's get this visit over with."

Old man Crowe was sitting on his porch flanked by two cowhands when the three Newman men rode up. "Don't bother getting down," he said. "You ain't welcome here. State your business."

"My son Aubrey's missing," said Hiram. "The last he was seen he was setting beside that new fence of yours looking across. Two of the last men to see him were riders of yours."

"That was us," said one of the cowhands on the porch.

"We seen him all right. Had a little visit," said the other. "His brother was with him. Still was when we rode off."

"Do you know anything about him, Crowe?" Hiram asked.

"Don't know a damn thing," said Crowe. "You can ride on out now."

Just then Hobbs came riding in. Crowe's face betrayed surprise. "What are you doing back so soon?" he demanded.

"I been robbed," Hobbs said.

"What? How?"

"I was riding along headed toward town when someone threw a rope around me. Jerked me from the saddle. Before I could do anything, he was on me. Had a gun in my ear. He tuck— Well, you know what he tuck."

"God damn it," said old Crowe. "You couldn't defend yourself against one man?"

"I never even seen him," said Hobbs.

Crowe got a suddenly suspicious look on his face. He looked at the three Newman riders and then back at Hobbs. "Could it a been one of these three?" he said.

"I don't see how," Hobbs said. "I passed them on the road. They said they was coming to see you. Said Aubrey was missing."

"We got to make sure," said Crowe. "Search them, boys."

The two cowhands on the porch stood up. Joe Croy reached for his gun, but Hiram stopped him. "Let them," he said.

"Get down off your horses," said one of the cowhands.

Hiram dismounted, and the two Croys followed him. While the two cowhands searched the three Newman riders thoroughly, Hobbs went through their saddlebags. At last one of the cowhands looked up at Crowe. "Nothing," he said. Hobbs shook his head.

"You men get on out of here," said Crowe, "and don't bother coming back."

• • •

Slocum and Bartley rode into Coffeyville. They rode the length of the street checking the horses tied to the hitch rails. They did not recognize any of them. "Let's check the saloon," Slocum said.

"His horse ain't here," said Bartley.

"Let's check it anyhow."

They hitched their horses and went inside. Looking around, they did not see anyone of note. They turned to go back out just as Silly Sally came into the room. "Bartley," she called out.

Bartley and Slocum turned to face her, and she came over to them.

"Hey, Silly Sally," Bartley said. "Look, I'm kind of in a hurry here."

"Aubrey's in the jailhouse," she said. "I don't know why. Me and Aubrey just came downstairs, and Clive Thornton met us at the bottom of the stairway with a gun in his hand. He took Aubrey with him."

"Let's go," said Slocum.

They hurried outside and down the street toward the jail. Just as they left the saloon, one of Slick Hannah's men came downstairs. He ordered a cup of coffee from Ernie, then strolled to the door to have a look outside. He was astonished to see the big Appaloosa at the hitch rail. He turned back inside and looked around the big room, half expecting to see the horse's owner there, but he did not. Ernie put the coffee on the bar, but the man was already rushing back upstairs.

Down at the jail, Slocum and Bartley found the sheriff sitting at his desk and Aubrey sitting in a jail cell. Thornton looked up.

"Well, well," he said. "Why ain't I surprised to find you running with the Newmans?"

"You got me there, Sheriff," said Slocum.

"Why's my brother in jail?" said Bartley.

"Suspicion," said Thornton.

"Suspicion of what?" Slocum asked.

"Stagecoach robbery," said Thornton.

"You got any proof," said Bartley, "or do you suspicion him just on account of you don't like us?"

"I got no proof yet," said Thornton, "but I'll get it."

"If you don't have any proof right now," said Slocum, "then I think you ought to let him go 'til you get some."

"That ain't for you to say."

"Well, I'm saying it. Unless you want me to go to the town council. Or does this town have one? Is this a one-man town?"

"We have a council," said Thornton.

"They must already be wondering about you," Slocum said. "You had a stagecoach robbery, and you ain't caught anyone yet. The loot was returned while you and your posse was limping back to town. A preacher got beaten to death just the other night. Now you have a man in your jail on suspicion without any proof of anything against him." He turned to Bartley. "What do they have here," he said, "a mayor?"

"Just hold on there," said Thornton. "I tossed Aubrey in here last night on account of he was too drunk to stand up. Yeah, I does suspect him of the stage robbery, but that ain't why I was holding him. You can go on ahead and take him home."

Thornton got up, took the keys, and walked to the cell. As he was unlocking the door, Bartley said, "Where's his horse?"

"Down in the livery," said Thornton. "He can pick him up. No charge."

Aubrey got out of the cell, and Thornton went back to his desk for Aubrey's gun. He handed the rig over to Aubrey, who strapped it on. "Let's get out of here," he said.

They walked back down the street to the saloon and picked up Bartley's and Slocum's horses, then walked on to the livery stable. They got Aubrey's horse, and the three mounted up.

"We got to get back to the house," said Slocum. "Everyone's worried about you out there."

As they rode out of town, they went past the saloon one more time. Slick and all of his men were gathered around the front door and the window watching. Ziggie said, "What do we do, boss? He's getting away."

"Someone has to follow him," Slick said.

"How?" said Ziggie.

Just then Calvin Black walked into the room. Slick grabbed him by the shoulder and dragged him to the front door. He shoved him through the door onto the sidewalk and pointed after Slocum and the two Newman brothers.

"There he is," Slick said. "Follow him. Find out where the hell he's going."

"I don't need to," said Calvin. "Them two with him are the Newman brothers. I'd say he's headed to the Newman ranch."

11

"Chief," said Tobe, standing at the window of their hotel room, "Hannah sure did seem interested in those three cowboys."

"He did, didn't he?" responded Johnson. "I wonder what's up."

"I'd say the cowboys know something about the Glitch woman."

"And I'd say you're right. Tobe, go get us that buggy, and bring it around to the back."

"You got some cowboys working for you?" Slick asked Calvin Black.

"I got a couple of boys that can ride," said Black.

"Can they handle themselves in a fight?"

"They're pretty good hands."

"Then get hold of them, and send them out to that ranch to get that woman."

Black felt like telling Slick to go to hell. Slick had never offered to pay him anything. He had threatened him. And Black was afraid of Slick. He had felt a little of what

Slick's man Ziggie could do. He didn't want to feel more. He considered having his boys shoot the whole gang, but then, there were eight in Slick Hannah's gang, and Black wasn't at all sure that he had enough good men to handle that. "Sure," he said. Black went over to the bar to talk to Ernie. "I want you to get a couple of the boys. Then I want the three of you to ride out to the Newman place. There's a woman out there. I'm sure of it. Not old lady Newman, but another woman. Good-looking. She's a city gal. I want you to grab her if you can. If you can't do it, figure out the lay of the land and get back here to tell me about it."

Ernie pulled off his apron and left the saloon. Black moved behind the counter to take over.

Slocum and the Newman brothers rode slowly on their way back to the ranch. As they rode, they talked. "So you were pretty drunk last night, huh?" Slocum asked.

"I guess so," said Aubrey.

"Does Thornton usually toss men in jail for that?"

"Hardly ever," said Bartley. "Not unless they're fighting or shooting up the place or something like that."

"Were you doing anything like that?" Slocum asked Aubrey.

"Hell, no," Aubrey said. "I'd just been upstairs with ole Silly Sally, you know? We come down the stairs and there he was. He pulled down on me and told me to come along."

"Did he say why?"

"Nope," said Aubrey, but Slocum noticed that Aubrey's head was hanging as he said it.

"Aubrey, I know you held up the stage."

"What?" Aubrey said.

"What makes you think you could know a thing like that?" said Bartley.

"Agnes recognized you," Slocum said. "She told me. And I expect that you were one of them too, Bartley, and the rest of the boys were your boys from the ranch. The number's right."

"What do you mean to do about it?" Aubrey asked.

"I ain't going to do nothing about it," Slocum said. "I ain't a lawman. Besides, you give everything back. Didn't you?"

"Well, yeah. We— We did."

Aubrey corrected his brother. "We give it all back except for one package, an envelope sort of. It was addressed to ole Thornton. It had money in it. I got no proof, but I'd bet anything it was from that son of a bitch John Crowe."

"You see, Slocum," said Bartley, "ole Crowe swindled us out of some land that had good water on it. We ain't exactly sure how they done it. We think that maybe Thornton done something with the papers in the county office. Anyhow, Thornton helped him, and Crowe's paying him off."

"Trying to," said Aubrey. His tone of voice changed with his next comment. "You were right, Slocum. He never tossed me in the can on account of me being drunk. He tried to get me to admit that I stole his money."

"What were you trying to do, Aubrey?" said Slocum. "Get even?"

"Well, yeah. Sort of. Get even some. Embarrass Thornton. You know, show him up. And then too, if he really goes after me, he might reveal where the money came from and why. Another thing, I figure he'll try to make ole Crowe pay him again, since he never seen the money."

"You're taking a hell of a chance, but it just might work," Slocum said. "Hell, I figured you boys had a pretty good reason for doing what you done."

Riding back from Crowe's ranch, Isaac Croy stopped his horse and dismounted. As he stepped to a flat rock beside the road, Hiram Newman said, "What the hell are you doing, Isaac? You been acting mighty strange."

Isaac tipped the big rock over and picked up a flat package that was lying underneath it. He walked to Hiram's horse and held the package up for Hiram. Hiram took it and saw the name written on it. "Sheriff Clive Thornton."

"What's this?" he said.

"Open it up," said Isaac.

"It's got Clive's name on it," Hiram said.

"Yeah," said Isaac. "And it's from ole man Crowe. Open it up."

Somewhat reluctantly, Hiram opened the package. His eyes opened wide as he saw the contents. Money. Lots of money in new bills.

"What's Crowe doing sending money to Thornton?" he said.

"On account of Thornton helped him grab that land," said Isaac.

"How do you know this is from Crowe?"

"I took it off Hobbs."

"So that's where you went a while ago."

"Yessir. I seen the package sticking out of his coat pocket, and I figured that was what it would be."

"What am I supposed to do with this money?"

"Just hang on to it, I guess," said Isaac. "Keep it out of Thornton's hands. Something'll happen."

• • •

Slocum and the Newman brothers arrived back at the house first. Maudie fussed over Aubrey for a spell. When she finally stopped, the three men sat on the porch. Maudie brought them out a bottle of whiskey and three glasses. In a few minutes, Agnes joined them, bringing her own glass. While they were sitting and talking, Hiram and the Croy brothers rode up. It wasn't long before they were joined by cousin Finis and cousin George. Hiram talked about the money that Isaac had nabbed from Hobbs. Slocum looked at Aubrey.

"You going to tell him the rest of the story?" he asked.

"Well, I—"

"You're all in this together," Slocum said.

"Yeah," said Aubrey. "Okay. Pop, it was us that robbed the stage the other day. We give everything back that we tuck, everything except one package. It was identical to that one."

"So Thornton didn't get his payment, and he demanded another one," said Hiram.

"That's what it looks like," Aubrey said.

"When he don't get this one, he's going to be really pissed off," Bartley said. The rest of the boys laughed, but Hiram sat with a sober expression on his face.

"I never thought I raised highwaymen," he said.

"So what?" said Aubrey. "What are you going to do? Turn us in?"

"Don't get to fighting among yourselves," Slocum said. "Hiram, I think the boys did the right thing. It looks to me like they might just flush ole Thornton out this way. When he don't get this money, he'll go back to Crowe for more. Crowe's going to get tired of paying for the same thing over and over again."

"We didn't take anything from anyone but Thornton," Aubrey said.

Hiram grumbled, "Well, maybe you're right, Slocum." Then he turned on Aubrey. "But the next time you get a harebrained idea, come to me with it before you do anything about it. You hear me?"

"I hear you, Pop, and I will."

The buggy lurched around the corner from the road onto the long drive that went up to the Newmans' main house. The people on the porch saw it coming. It was almost comical, bouncing and lurching, being driven way too fast for the dirt trail it was on. Hiram stood up to look. "Who's that coming?" he said.

As it came closer, Aubrey said, "It looks like dudes."

"That one's dressed like a farmer," said Bartley.

"He still looks like a dude," said Aubrey as Agnes got up and hurried into the house.

Slocum stood and walked over to wait at the top of the stairs that went up to the porch. "Be ready for anything, boys," he said as the buggy rolled on up to near the porch and stopped. Johnson started to get out.

"Hold on there," said Hiram. "You ain't been invited to light." Johnson settled back down. "Who are you," said Hiram, "and what do you want here?"

"My name's Johnson. I'm the chief of police in St. Louis." He reached inside his coat pocket.

"Keep your hand out of there," said Hiram.

Carefully, Johnson pulled out his coat to show that he had no gun there. "I'm just going for my credentials," he said.

"Go on then," said Hiram.

Johnson pulled out an identification card and a badge and held them out to show Hiram. "This is Sergeant Tobe," he said.

Tobe fished his credentials and badge out of the pocket in the bib of the overalls.

"So that's who you are," said Hiram. "Now, what do you want here?"

"Can we get down out of this buggy?" Johnson asked.

Hiram looked at Slocum, and Slocum nodded.

"Come on," said Hiram.

Johnson and Tobe dismounted the buggy. Tobe stretched and groaned.

"We're looking for a woman who left St. Louis in a big hurry. We followed her out here to Coffeyville," Johnson said. "We have reason to believe that she might be here with you."

"What do you want her for?" Hiram asked.

"She's a witness to a murder that was done in St. Louis," said Johnson. "The killer and his gang followed her too. They mean to get to her before I do and kill her to keep her from testifying in court. I want her for a witness, and I want to keep her safe from the gang."

"How many men are in this gang?" Slocum asked.

"Eight of them followed the woman," Johnson said.

"There's just two of you," said Slocum. "How you going to protect anyone from eight gangsters?"

"We got no strange women out here," said Hiram. "You can go on your way now."

"Look," said Johnson. "We have the woman's safety in mind. We have to—"

"You never answered my question," said Slocum. "How are the two of you going to keep her safe?"

"Don't worry about that, cowboy," said Tobe. "We'll manage all right."

"Let them come up and take a seat, Hiram," Slocum said.

"All right."

Slocum motioned them to climb the stairs and take seats, and they did. "Let me ask you some questions," Slocum said. "Suppose the woman was here. Just suppose. Wouldn't she be better off staying right here where she's got plenty of protection 'til you had those men behind bars?"

"I got nothing right now to arrest them for," said Johnson. "Besides that, I'm way beyond my jurisdiction. I can't arrest anyone out here."

"Then you couldn't force the woman to go back with you even if you found her?"

"I was hoping that we could persuade her," Johnson said.

"If I was the woman," Slocum said, "I'd say, I ain't going all the way back to St. Looie with just you two men when there's eight men out there looking for me to kill me."

"I guess that's a possibility," Johnson said.

"Hiram," said Slocum, "do you have room for two more in the bunkhouse?"

"Well, yeah. I guess so."

"Why don't you gents stay out here?" Slocum said. "You never know what might turn up."

"If the woman isn't here," said Johnson, "there's no point in it, is there? And those eight men are in town. We can keep an eye on them there."

Slocum opened the door and poked his head inside. "Agnes," he said, "would you come here please?"

Out on the road, Ernie and two other men were just getting off their horses near the gate.

12

Ernie and his two cronies sneaked in on foot 'til they were close enough that they could see the house, the porch, and who all was sitting on the porch.

"I recognize the whole Newman bunch," said one of the cowboys, "and that fellow that rides the spotty-ass horse. I don't know them other two. The one in the city suit and the one in the overalls. There's a gal there that I don't know."

"She's the one we're interested in," said Ernie. "She's the one the boss wants us to snatch."

"There's nine men on that porch," said the shortest of the two cowboys. "How the hell are we going to snatch anyone?"

"Let's go back to town and tell the boss," said Ernie. "Let him know what the odds are like out here."

Thornton stormed into the saloon. "Give me a whiskey, Calvin," he said, seeing Black behind the bar. "Where's Ernie?"

"I sent him on an errand," said Black, pouring the sheriff's drink.

Thornton picked it up and turned it down. Slamming the glass down, he said, “Another one.” Black poured it.

“Something eating at you, Clive?” he said.

“Damn right.”

“Well, what is it?”

“I can’t talk about it,” said Thornton.

Black looked up toward a table full of city slickers. If he spoke low, they wouldn’t be able to make out his words.

“Something’s eating me too,” he said, “and I can’t talk about it.”

Thornton glanced over his shoulder and saw the table of dudes. He nodded. Some of them nodded back, and others murmured greetings. Thornton turned back to Black. “Why can’t you talk about it?” he said.

“They’ll kill me.”

“Do they ever go up to their rooms?”

“Sometimes.”

“When they do, come and see me.”

He tossed down his second drink and left the saloon.

“Hey, Calvin,” Slick called out. “Bring us another bottle.”

It was late in the afternoon when Ernie and his two cohorts got back to town and went into the saloon. No one was there but Black and the Hannah gang.

“What’d you find out?” Black blurted out anxiously.

“Come on over here,” called Slick.

Black hurried from behind the counter, and Ernie and the cowhands moved to the Hannah gang’s table. “Well,” said Slick, “what’d you find out?”

“The gal’s there,” said Ernie.

“There where?” said Slick.

“At the Newman ranch. I saw her on the porch.”

"Whyn't you snatch her?" said Slick.

"There was nine men on the porch with her," Ernie said. "We wouldn't a had a chance, the three of us."

"I guess you're right," Slick said. "All right. Let me think about it. I'll come up with a plan. We'll do it tomorrow. In the meantime, I want you three to keep your eyes on the place in case she tries to leave. You got that?"

"Sure," said Ernie.

Slick Hannah got up, and so did the rest of the gang. They followed him upstairs. As soon as they were gone, Ernie said, "Boss?"

"Yeah?" said Black.

"What do you want us to do?"

"I want you to get back behind the bar," Black said. "You other two boys, do what the man said. Get out there and keep your eyes open."

"Okay," the short cowboy said. The two turned and left the saloon, and Ernie went back to work behind the bar. Black hurried outside, then down the street to the sheriff's office. When he burst through the door, Thornton looked up from behind his desk.

"They leave?" he asked.

"They went upstairs," said Black. "Listen to me. I met a gal on the stage. A good-looking gal. City gal. I tried to get along with her, you know, but she never showed no interest. Then that Slocum showed up at the depot, and she went off with him. It pissed me off.

"Anyhow, those city dudes showed up later, and they was looking for the gal. The same gal. I could tell by the way they described her. I told them I might know something and asked them what it was worth to them. Well, the boss, that Slick, and his next in line, the one they call Ziggie, got me back in my office and beat the shit out of me. They said I'd better tell them what I knew or else. So I been helping them. If I don't, they'll kill me."

"We can't have shit like that going on here in Coffeyville," Thornton said.

"What'll you do?" said Black. "There's eight of them."

"Yeah," Thornton said. "We'll need a good-sized posse to be sure. I wonder if I could get ole Crowe to join it."

"Crowe? What for?"

"He's getting a little old," said Thornton, "but he's still a good gun hand. I think we could use him. Who've you got?"

"I've got Ernie," said Black, "and the two boys I sent out with him this morning."

"To do what?"

"I sent them out to the Newman ranch to look for that gal. She's out there. The Newmans and that goddamned Slocum are protecting her out there."

"The Newmans, huh?" Thornton said. "This is getting interesting."

"Interesting? How?" said Black. "What are you talking about?"

"Listen, Calvin," said Thornton. "We might could help each other out quite a bit. You spotted that gal, and the city gang is after her, and you're caught in the middle. Right?"

"That's right, and it ain't comforting."

"Just listen. I done a little job for old Crowe. It was against the Newmans, and he owes me for it. He says he sent my pay on the stage, but the stage got robbed."

"I thought the bandits returned all the loot," Black said.

"Not quite all," said Thornton. "I went out to see old Crowe and told him he still owes me. He said he'd take care of it, but I ain't seen nothing yet."

"Okay, but I don't get it. How can we help each other out?"

"We got to get those gangsters out to attack the Newman ranch," said Thornton. "I got to get a posse together pretending to help out against the gangsters. I need to get old Crowe with the posse. We get a big fight going out there, we might could get rid of— Who knows?"

"How will it help you to get Crowe killed?"

"It might not," said Thornton, "but it will give me some satisfaction. Then again, I think it was the Newmans what stole my money. If we was to get a shooting war going out at their place, I might stand a chance of getting it back some way. I ain't thought it all through quite yet, but I'm headed for it."

"All right," said Black. "All right. I think I get it. But all I need is to get rid of those city bastards. That's all I need."

"What about Slocum and the gal?"

Black sat in deep thought for a moment. "You're right," he said. "I'd sure be tickled to see that Slocum dead. Then I'd have me a chance to get that city woman. I sure would. What do you want me to do?"

"Just sit tight," said Thornton. "I'll contact you."

Black left the office, and Thornton scrunched up his brow in deep thought for a moment. Then he got up and strapped his gun around his waist, put on his hat, and left the office. He got his horse and headed out for the Crowe ranch.

• • •

"Slocum," said Johnson, "we can't just sit around out here doing nothing while Slick Hannah and his gang are right in town, getting ready to do who knows what."

"You said you can't arrest him, didn't you?" said Slocum.

"Well, yeah, but I could be in town watching him to see what he's up to."

"He most likely knows that Agnes is out here by now," Slocum said. "If he's out to protect himself against a murder charge, he'll make a move sometime soon. Men like that get bored fast, and I don't reckon that Coffeyville is much to his liking."

"What do you think he'll do?"

"I expect him to attack this ranch some way, and I expect it pretty damn soon."

"Well, then, shouldn't we be getting ready for it?"

"You're right, Chief. We should. You could put your man out there to watch the road."

"I'll do it," Johnson said.

Johnson got up to go find Tobe, and Slocum went looking for Aubrey. He found him at the corral.

"Aubrey," he said.

"Yeah?"

"I want you to send out some men and round up a bunch of your cattle. Gather them up over there behind that fence."

"What for?"

"Just do it, and then have all the men gather up around the house and the bunkhouse."

"It sounds to me like you're expecting some trouble."

"Always, Aubrey."

Aubrey called out to Joseph Croy who was not far away,

and the two of them went to round up the rest. Slocum walked back to the house.

At the saloon in town, Silly Sally was just about to go down the stairs, but she saw Slick Hannah and his gang huddled around a table. Her boss, Black, was with them, and so was Ernie. She didn't like the Hannah gang. For that matter, she didn't like Black or Ernie, but she had learned to put up with them. She turned to go back to her room, but something in the tones of the voices below made her stop. She stepped back against the wall where she would not be seen.

"To get to that woman," Black was saying, "we've got to have a bunch of men. There's at least ten men out there at that ranch, and they're just clustered around her protecting her."

"There's eight of us," said Slick, "and you and your three makes it twelve."

"How're we going to get out to a ranch, boss?" said Ziggie. "I can't ride no horse."

"Shut up, Ziggie," said Slick. "Could we take them with twelve?"

"It'd be chancy," Black said. "If we was to go riding into that ranch, we'd be out in the open. They'd be barricaded in the ranch house and maybe the bunkhouse. We'd be better off with more."

"How many more can you get?"

"I don't know. I think I might could get the sheriff and a posse to help us out."

"We don't want no sheriff," Ziggie said.

"Wait a minute," said Black.

"Shut up, Ziggie," said Slick. "Go on."

"Well," said Black, "the sheriff has got it in for the

Newmans. I ain't exactly sure why, but I don't think it would take much to get him to join in with us."

"I don't know about that," Slick said thoughtfully. "But how about this? Can you get him to round up his posse and go after the Newmans on his own and suggest that we could join in with his posse like the good citizens we are and help him out? Do you think you could manage that?"

"I could try," Black said. "I'd have to come up with some reason. I mean, I know he has it in for them, but he ain't got a legal reason to go after them. You know?"

"Didn't I hear something about a stagecoach robbery?" Slick said.

"Yeah."

"Can you pin that on the Newmans?"

"Well, I— Wait a minute. Yeah. I know how to do it." Black reached into his pocket and produced the medal that Ernie had taken from around the preacher's neck.

"What's that?" Slick asked.

"There was a preacher on that stage," said Black. "This belonged to him. I'll tell the sheriff that I found it in the room upstairs after Aubrey Newman left. "That'll be all the proof he needs."

Upstairs, Silly Sally ran to her room. Quickly, she changed her clothes. Dressed in riding gear, she went to the far end of the hall and stepped out on an outside landing. She hurried down the stairs and ran as fast as she could to the livery stable.

13

Crowe was aggravated to see Thornton again so soon, but he offered him a comfortable seat in his large living room and poured him a big glass full of good brown whiskey. He poured one for himself and sat down across the room.

"I know why you're here," he said. "The money never got to you. I sent it with Hobbs yesterday, but somebody jumped him on the road and stole it. Now I know what you're going to say. You're going to say that twice I told you I sent the money and twice I said somebody stole it. It sounds fishy, but it's the truth."

Thornton took a big swallow of the whiskey and relished it as it burned its way down his gullet. "You got any cash around the house here?" he asked.

"Not that much."

"Well, give me what you've got. You can get the rest to me later."

Crowe groaned as he stood up from his easy chair. He walked to a big desk off to one side of the room and opened a drawer. He took something out of the desk, walked over to Thornton, and handed him a stack of bills.

Thornton thumbed through them. "That all you got?" he said.

"It's all I've got here," Crowe said.

"Well, you get the rest to me as soon as you can. Now, I've got a proposition for you. I think I know who stole your money. Remember it was your money on account of it never got into my hands. I think I know who stole it, and I know how you can get it back and a whole lot more to boot."

"I'm listening," Crowe said.

"I believe that it was the Newman bunch what robbed the stage, and I'd bet money it was one of them that jumped your man Hobbs and stole that other money."

"Go on."

"I mean to form a posse and ride out to their ranch. I want you and some of your boys to join in with me."

"I'm too old to ride in a posse," Crowe said.

"You can still ride and you can still shoot. Listen, if you'll do what I'm asking, I'll forget the rest of the money you owe me. I'll forget it at least until we find what was stole."

"You mean to arrest the whole Newman crew?"

"I mean to kill them all," said Thornton. "Then their whole ranch would be up for grabs."

"I, uh, I don't know about that," Crowe said. "That would be mass murder."

"Not if they're resisting arrest," the sheriff said.

"I'll give you 'til the day after tomorrow," Thornton said. "Then you show up with your boys in town first thing in the morning. I'll have a posse ready, and we'll all head out to the Newman place. Be there."

He stood up and walked toward the door. Crowe reached under his vest and brought out a small Navy Colt. He thumbed back the hammer and pulled the trigger. The shot hit Thornton between the shoulder blades. He wrenched and twisted his body, turning toward old man Crowe with a painful and angry grimace on his face as he reached for his own weapon. Crowe fired again, this bullet smacking into Thornton's forehead. Thornton fell back against the door and slid slowly to the floor. He lay still there, dead.

Crowe put his pistol away and hurried over to the body. Bending down, he took his money back. Then he stood and dragged the body away just enough so he could open the door. He stepped out on the porch and looked around. He saw one of his trusted hands out by the barn, and he called out to him. The man came sauntering over to the house and mounted the porch steps. Crowe had already gone back into the house, so the cowhand stepped in too.

He stopped and stared at the body on the floor and the blood pooling around it. His eyes were wide. His face showed astonishment.

"What happened, boss?" he finally said.

"Drag him out there and throw him across his saddle," said Crowe. "Ride out to the road with him and dump him somewhere out there. Go on now."

Tobe walked out toward the gate to the Newman ranch where he was going to take up his new sentry duty. He wasn't sure what he would be watching for. He guessed a bunch of riders, but he couldn't imagine the Hannah gang on horseback. Out on the road, on the other side, sort of hidden in the brush, Black's two cowhands were lounging.

"This here's the easiest job I ever had," said one.

"It's boring as hell," said the other. "I'd rather be in the saloon having a drink."

"Or two or three."

"Yeah."

"We're just wasting our time here. What the hell are we watching for anyhow?"

"For that city gal. In case she tries to leave."

"Oh, yeah."

They heard some footsteps and stood up quickly. Looking in the direction of the gate, they saw a man looking uncomfortable in a pair of brand-new overalls. He saw them at the same time.

"Hey," said Tobe. "What are you doing here?"

One of the men jerked out his revolver and fired, the bullet smashing into Tobe's chest. Tobe staggered, pulling his own police revolver out from under the bib of the overalls. As the two men ran for their horses, Tobe fired, hitting one in the back, but the other one disappeared. Tobe grabbed on to the upright post of the gateway. Slowly he slid to the ground.

They heard the shots at the house. Slocum and Aubrey were the first at the scene, but Chief Johnson was not far behind. The chief rushed to the side of his sergeant. Tobe was breathing heavily. Johnson lifted up his head. "Tobe," he said, "take it easy. We'll fix you up. You'll get through this."

"No," said Tobe, between gasping breaths. "No. I don't think so. I think I'm done for. Sorry I let you down, Chief."

"Don't even think that, old man. You didn't let me down."

"You got to do it by yourself now, Chief."

"Who was it, Tobe? Do you know?"

"Two cowboys. I think I got one of them."

"I'll find the other one and get him for you," Johnson said.

Slocum and Audrey were across the road, and Slocum found the body of the one cowhand. Aubrey walked over to join him. "I know him," Aubrey said. "Well, sort of. He works off and on for Calvin Black."

"The saloon owner?" said Slocum.

"Yeah. Him. He usually has another guy with him. I don't know his name, but I know him when I see him."

"Let's go back across and see how Tobe is doing," Slocum said. "This one's deader'n hell."

When they crossed the road, Johnson was standing up, his hat in his hand. "He's gone," he said. "He told me it was two cowboys."

"Well," said Slocum, "he got one of them."

"I'll get the other one," said Johnson.

"I can damn sure point him out to you," Aubrey said.

"When do we move, Calvin?" said Slick. "I've wasted enough time in this place."

"The sheriff said he'd let me know," Black said. "He's getting a posse together."

"Well, we can't wait much longer. I got to get that gal and get my ass back to St. Louis. I've got business interests there. Big business. It needs my attention."

The cowboy who had escaped from Tobe came into the saloon. He hurried over to the table where his boss and the Hannah gang were sitting.

"What are you doing back here?" Black said.

"Some guy in overalls came out to the road," the man said. "He hollered at us and Melvin fired a shot. The guy shot Melvin and killed him. I got the hell out of there."

"A guy in overalls?" Black said.

"Yeah. He was dressed like a farmer, but he didn't look right to me."

"What do you mean?"

"He just didn't look like he belonged in them clothes. They looked new too."

"Where would a guy buy clothes like that?" said Slick.

"Just down the street at the general store," Black said.

"Ziggie," said Slick, "take this rube here with you and go down to the general store. See if you can find out who bought them new farmer clothes."

"Sure thing, boss," Ziggie said. He stood up and gestured at the cowhand. "Come on, rube," he said.

The two of them walked out of the saloon.

Silly Sally turned her horse into the lane that led up to the Newman house. She was still riding fast when she reached the porch, and she brought the horse to a fast stop, sending up clouds of dust. Slocum was sitting on the porch with Aubrey.

"Silly Sally," said Aubrey, "what brings you way out here?"

Silly Sally dismounted and ran up the stairs. She was panting. Aubrey gestured toward a chair, and she sat down. "I heard something," she said. "Calvin was talking with those dudes, you know, the ones that's staying in his saloon."

"That's Slick Hannah and his gang," Slocum said.

"Yeah," said Silly Sally. "That's his name. Slick. Calvin was talking to them. I was upstairs, and I could hear what they was saying, but they didn't see me. They was trying to figure out how to attack you all out here. The city guys said they couldn't ride horses. That Slick, he said that he needed to get that gal. I don't know who he was talking about, but they mentioned the Newmans, all of you," she said, looking at Aubrey, "and they mentioned someone named Slocum."

"I'm Slocum."

"Oh, yeah. Well, they mentioned you too. They mean to kill everyone. Crowe wants the ranch."

"Crowe?" said Aubrey. "Was he there?"

"No, but Calvin said that Thornton could get him in on it."

"Whoa," said Aubrey. "Slow down. Are you saying that Black, and the Hannah gang, and Crowe and Thornton are all in this together?"

"That's sure what it sounded like," said Silly Sally. "They're going to all get together and call it a posse and come out here to kill you all. Oh, yeah. Their excuse is going to be that you killed that preacher."

"Me?" said Aubrey.

"Yeah. On account of Calvin was on the stage whenever it got robbed, and he seen a thing the preacher was wearing around his neck. The robbers took it, but then they give everything back, and the preacher was wearing it again the other night, but when they found his body, it was gone. Well, Calvin had it. He took it away from Ernie. They mean to say they found it on you."

"So Ernie killed the preacher," Aubrey said.

"Seems likely," said Slocum.

"So what are you going to do?" asked Silly Sally.

"We're already doing it," Slocum said, "but it's good to know who all will be involved in this thing."

"They ain't going to wipe us out," Aubrey said.

"Let's go tell your old man," said Slocum.

"I guess I'll be getting back," said Silly Sally. "I just thought that you all had ought to know the worst."

"You ain't going back, Silly Sally," said Aubrey. "It might not be safe for you. You're going to stay here with us 'til this thing is all cleared up."

"But my job—"

"When we're all done with this, your boss will be dead."

"Where's that goddamned sheriff?" asked Slick.

"I don't know," said Black. "He just told me to sit tight and wait for him. Said he'd let me know when we would be ready."

"Well, go find him and bring him here. Right now."

Black left the saloon just as Ziggie and the cowboy returned. They went to the table to join Slick and the rest of the gang.

"What'd you find out?" Slick demanded.

"No names," said Ziggie, "but the fellow in the store remembered selling the outfit to someone, he said, was dressed kind of like me. A dude, he said. A city fellow."

Slick wrinkled his brow. "A city fellow?" he said. "What the hell would a city guy be doing out at the Newman ranch? And how come a city fellow would buy an outfit like that anyhow?"

"It musta been a disguise, boss," said Ziggie.

"A disguise? A disguise, yeah. Yeah. He dressed up so we wouldn't think nothing about it if we seen him. He's a cop, Ziggie. The goddamned cops has followed us from St. Louis. Shit."

14

Slocum had the Newman cowhands build a wall around the house with bales of hay. They still kept someone on sentry duty out by the gate. Everyone had orders to keep his guns loaded and ready. Slocum was taking no chances, and no one disagreed with him either. They meant to be ready for a small war, whenever it came.

"All bets are off," Slocum said to Hiram Newman. "Your sheriff has thrown in with the outlaws, and we're on our own."

Agnes, having heard the order for everyone to keep his weapons ready, secretly pulled the Merwin and Hulbert Company pocket pistol out and checked it over. Then she tucked it back into her purse. Rifles and shotguns were stashed around at convenient locations, all cleaned, oiled, and loaded. All was in readiness.

Calvin Black had gone looking for Sheriff Thornton with no success. When he had returned to the saloon to report his failure, Slick Hannah had ordered him to ride out to the Crowe ranch himself to recruit old man Crowe, so Black was reluctantly riding out to the Crowe place, grumbling all the way. He did not like taking orders from Hannah, but he was afraid not to. He feared for his life, and Thornton had already indicated that he would do nothing to help Black in this situation. Instead he had schemed up his super-posse notion. He intended to get rid of everyone who was any kind of problem for himself or for Black in the course of the big fight that was planned. Black was not at all sure that they could manage to kill off the Hannah gang, Crowe, Slocum, and the Newmans. That was a hell of a chore. He did not trust Thornton, but for the time being, he had no choice but to go along with him.

He wasn't at all sure what he would say to Crowe either. Was he supposed to ask the old man if Thornton had been to see him? If so, was he supposed to ask about the conversation they'd had? What if Crowe's answer was that Thornton had not been there? Was he then supposed to try to recruit Crowe and his hands for the super-posse himself? And if he did so, what would Thornton say about Black's having gone over his head, so to speak? He had so damn many questions in his head that it was spinning.

He cursed the day that the Hannah gang had ridden into Coffeyville. He wished that he had never seen them. He wished that he had not been on the stagecoach with that goddamned Glitch woman. If he had never seen her, the gang would have no reason to hang around him and keep using him for their dirty work. He wished— But wishing was doing him no good now.

He had a couple of miles to go to reach the Crowe ranch when he saw the body. He dismounted to check it and was astonished to find Sheriff Clive Thornton with a bullet in the back and another in the head. He checked the sheriff's pockets and found no cash, but he took the six-gun—he wasn't sure why. In a state of near panic, Black wondered what he should do. He wondered if Thornton had made it to see Crowe and had been ambushed and killed out on the road by someone unknown, or if he had never made it to see Crowe but had been killed on his way to the Crowe ranch.

He wondered if he should go on to see Crowe and try to find out, or if he should simply ride back to Coffeyville with the body and the news and tell Slick Hannah that the deal with Crowe had not worked out. Thornton was dead. But if he should do that, there was no telling what Slick would scheme up next, what he would tell Black to do. Suddenly, a thought occurred to him. What if he should just disappear? Ride away and not return to Coffeyville? Slick would have to proceed on his own. He would not hang around Coffeyville forever. Black already knew that. The Hannah gang, including Slick himself, was already tiring of the small town.

Black could escape, stay away for a while, long enough for the Hannah gang to get the hell out, and then return to his business. He decided that was what he would do. He would not go to see Crowe. He would not return to Coffeyville. He would not carry the dead sheriff and the news back to town. He would just get the hell out for a while. He climbed back on his horse and rode straight ahead fast.

Agnes and Silly Sally sat on the porch alone drinking coffee. Silly Sally was still dressed in her riding clothes, and Agnes had no idea what the girl did for a living. She seemed personable enough though. They had not been formally introduced, but Agnes had heard that the girl had brought them some important news.

"I want to thank you for helping out," Agnes said.

"Oh, it wasn't no trouble," said Silly Sally. "I just overheard something, and I come out here to tell Aubrey about it."

"I understand it was pretty important," said Agnes.

"Well, I guess so. There's a whole bunch of them ganging up on the Newmans."

"What's going on around here anyway, Sally?" Agnes said.

"Oh, please, my name is Silly Sally."

"Very well. What's going on around here, Silly Sally?"

"Well, there's that bunch of city gangsters after you."

"I know that, of course," said Agnes. "But what's the trouble with the Newmans?"

"A man named Crowe, which is a big rancher whose place is right next to the Newmans' place got his hands on some of their land. The land has got good grazing and good water on it. The rumor is that Sheriff Thornton helped Crowe get it. Something about papers in the county records or something. Anyhow, I guess the Newmans are out to get even with the sheriff and Crowe, or something."

"Where does your boss figure into this?"

"Oh, that one's easy," said Silly Sally. "He wants you. Same as those city gangsters, except I guess his reasons are different. Anyhow, he let them know he knew you, and they've been using him ever since. They got him scared to death, I can tell you."

"Oh," said Agnes. "It's all very confusing, but I think I'm beginning to get a grip on it."

Carl George was old man Crowe's foreman. He had been into Coffeyville on business and stopped by Black's saloon for a drink. It seemed to Carl George that everywhere he went in town, people were talking about the mysterious city woman who was staying with the Newmans; the stagecoach robbery; the stranger who had the look of a gunfighter, who was also staying with the Newmans; the city gangsters who had come to town, it seemed to stay, at least long enough to get their hands on the city woman who was staying with the Newmans; and some shady connection between Crowe and Thornton, having something to do with the land that Crowe had gotten away from the Newmans. It also seemed that public sympathy was on the side of the Newmans. As soon as he got back to the ranch, he stopped at the big house to have a talk with his boss.

"So the folks are siding with the Newmans, are they?" said Crowe. "Well, give it some time, and they'll change their tune. The public has a short memory, and they're fickle. Remember that, Carl George."

"Yes, sir. There's talk too that the city gang is planning to attack the Newman ranch."

"I know all about that," Crowe said. "That goddamned bastard Thornton was trying to make me join in on that deal. That's why I killed him."

"The way I see it is that gang just only wants that gal that's out there. That city gal, you know. Once they get her, they'll go back where they come from."

"Leaving a bunch of witnesses to what they done?" said Crowe.

Carl George scratched his head and thought about that. "Well, I guess you're right. They wouldn't want that, would they?"

"We're just staying the hell out of it, Carl George," said Crowe. "We don't have any fight with the Newmans. I don't want their goddamned ranch. I've already got the only piece of it I wanted. I got nothing against the Newmans, and I never even set eyes on any of them city folks. Leave it alone, Carl George. It'll all go away."

"Ernie," Slick Hannah shouted. "Where the hell's your boss?"

"I don't know, Mr. Hannah," Ernie said. "The last I knew he had rode out toward the Crowe place to have a talk with old man Crowe on account of he couldn't find Clive Thornton. I ain't seen him since then."

"Well, we got to get something going here. I'm sick of all this waiting around. I want you to get a buggy to take me and Ziggie out to this Crowe place."

"Now?"

"Right now."

It seems that all things were converging on old Crowe. Slocum had also decided to have a talk with Crowe. He mounted his Appaloosa and rode across the Newman ranch, the Appaloosa leaping the wire fence easily when they came to it. Riding across the range that Crowe had bilked the Newmans out of, he encountered some of Crowe's riders. They met him with guns in their hands.

Slocum stopped the Appaloosa and raised his own hands about shoulder high. When the riders were close enough, he said, "I'm not looking for any trouble here."

"It looks like trouble when you come riding across our range," said one rider.

"From the Newman place," said another.

"I want to have a visit with your boss," said Slocum. "This is the closest way."

"What do you want to visit about?"

"I reckon that's between me and him."

"You ain't getting past us unless you got a damn good reason."

"Does he know you're coming? Is he expecting you?"

"He ain't expecting me," Slocum said.

"Get down offa that spotty-ass horse," said one, thumbing back the hammer on his six-gun.

Slocum looked at the men, all with guns in hands. The odds were not good. He dismounted. One of the cowhands rode around behind him and tossed a loop, catching him around the arms. He pulled it tight. Another rode up quickly, knocking Slocum down with the side of his horse as he passed him by. Then they were all off their horses, all but the man with the rope who kept his horse backing slowly away, keeping the rope tight. Slocum squirmed, but he was caught good.

A man kicked a glancing blow at his head. Another kicked him in the side, but the kick just caught him on the arm. Two men bent low to swing fists at his head, a few of the punches catching him pretty good along the side of the head. Then a boot heel caught him hard on top of the head, and everything went black. After that he knew nothing.

Ernie was driving the hack toward the Crowe place. He did not have much to say. He was wondering where the hell Calvin Black had gone, why he had not returned. He did not like taking orders from these city slickers, did not even like having them around. If he had his way, he would get the gal they were after and turn her over to them. What the hell did he care about her? She was nothing to him. It would have been well worth it to get rid of these bastards. He drove past the entrance to the Newman ranch on his way, and Slick Hannah saw the sign over the gateway.

"Newman," he said. "This is the Newman ranch?"

"That's what it says," Ernie answered.

"Don't get smart with me," said Slick.

"That's the Newman ranch," Ernie said.

"That's where they've got the woman?"

"That's what I understand."

"Yeah," said Slick. "Yeah. That's what your boss said. They got her out at the Newman ranch. Well, we'll be paying a visit out here real soon now. How much farther on to Crowe's place?"

"Just a few more miles down this road," said Ernie.

Slocum came to his senses slowly. He groaned out loud and tried to sit up, but something was wrong. His brain was not working at full capacity, so it took him a little while to figure out that his arms were tied tightly to his sides. He rolled around 'til he found a way he could stand up without using them. "Damn," he said. His head hurt, and he wanted to put a hand to it, but of course, he couldn't. He spat on the ground, and he saw that he was spitting blood. Standing uneasily on weak legs, he looked around. There was no one in sight. His horse was gone. He wondered if they had stolen it or just driven it away. Well, he hadn't much choice. He started walking back toward the Newman ranch. It promised to be a long and miserable walk.

15

Slocum staggered back toward the Newman ranch, stumbling and falling more than once. His head continued to hurt from the kicking it had received and both his arms hurt from bruises. He realized though that he was lucky there. His arms had been pinned to his sides by the rope, and they had protected his ribs from the vicious kicks. He could tell that his face was banged up a bit too, and his mouth must have been cut. He knew that from the blood he had spat.

He wasn't used to taking long walks, even when he was feeling well. His legs were tired, and then they began to hurt with each step. Still he kept plodding on until he came to the fence. The Appaloosa had taken it with ease, but Slocum had a different problem. He could not climb over it, not with his arms tied tight to his sides. It would be difficult to slip between the strands of barbed wire too. He might be able to do it, but he would most likely either scratch himself or get his clothes caught in the wire. Finally he decided to lie down on the ground and slither under the bottom wire.

It wasn't easy getting down on the ground. He had to squat until he fell into a sitting position. Then he lay back and scooted himself with his feet, pushing his body slowly underneath the wire. Then he had to go through the tedious process of getting back to his feet without the aid of his hands. He made it though. He continued his slow and painful way back to the Newman house. The sun was beating down on him with no mercy, and it did not help matters that he had lost his hat somewhere along the way, most likely when he had been lying on the ground being kicked and beaten. He had not had the time or inclination to think about it before, but now he missed his hat.

He stumbled into a small grove of trees, and he found the shade a great relief. Then he heard a familiar nicker. He stopped and looked around, then he called out. He heard the nicker again, and then the Appaloosa came walking through the trees. Slocum felt a tremendous sense of relief. The men must have chased the horse away, and it must have headed back toward the Newman ranch, leaping the fence once again, and then stopping to enjoy the shade in the grove of trees.

"Come on, old son," said Slocum.

The horse walked up to him and nuzzled him with its muzzle. Slocum sure did miss the use of his hands. His relief at finding his horse was dampened a bit by the knowledge that he could not mount without use of his hands. Even if he could get a foot in a stirrup, he would not be able to swing his body up and on the horse's back. He would fall on his ass if he tried it. Getting on the horse without hands would be a hell of a circus trick. Then a thought came to him. It would be worth a try.

He began talking to the horse and pushing against it

with his body, urging it to lie down. That was a trick he had taught the Appaloosa some years earlier, but he had used his hands and the reins. This was more difficult. The horse whinnied and stepped aside, not at all sure of what Slocum wanted it to do.

"I wish you could talk American, old horse," Slocum said. He continued pushing and urging the horse to lie down. At last it did, a bit awkwardly. It was on its side, and Slocum stepped over the saddle, nearly falling down again in the process. "Come on," he said. "Get up. Let's go now." The horse lurched to its feet with Slocum in the saddle. He got both feet into the stirrups and urged the horse toward the ranch house.

Ernie was driving the two gangsters out to the Crowe ranch when he spotted a body beside the road. He stopped the buggy and got out.

"What are you doing?" demanded Slick.

"There's a dead guy here," said Ernie.

"That ain't none of our business," Ziggie said.

Ernie walked over to the corpse and knelt down. It was lying on its face, but Ernie felt a sense of recognition. Gingerly, he took hold of a shoulder and rolled the body over.

"God damn," he said.

"What?" said Ziggie.

"Who is it?" said Slick.

"It's Clive Thornton," said Ernie.

"The sheriff?" said Slick.

"Yeah. Sheriff Clive Thornton. Somebody's shot him. Twice. Once in the back and then in the head. Somebody's killed Clive."

"Well," said Slick, "that explains how come your boss

never found him. It don't explain what the hell happened to your boss though."

"His gun's gone," said Ernie.

"Check his pockets," Slick ordered.

Ernie stuck his hands in all of Thornton's pockets but he came up empty. "I'd say he's been robbed too," he said.

"Well, it ain't our problem," said Slick. "Climb on back in here and let's get going."

"On to the Crowe ranch?" Ernie asked.

"That's where we was headed, ain't it? Come on."

"We ought to do something about Clive."

"We ain't putting no stiff in here with us," said Slick, "and we got business at the Crowe joint. Come on now."

The cowboys who had beaten Slocum rode back to the Crowe ranch house and found Carl George on the porch with old Crowe. They rode up laughing and dismounted, climbing the stairs to the porch.

"What the hell's so funny?" asked Crowe.

"You know that Slocum fellow?" asked one.

"I know who he is," said Crowe.

"What about him?" said Carl George.

"We just met him coming across our pasture. I guess he'd jumped the fence. Anyhow, we stopped him and asked him what the hell he was doing on our range."

A second cowhand interrupted. "He said he was coming to see you, boss, and we told him he couldn't do that."

"Well, we roped him off his horse, that spotty-ass horse he rides, and kicked him around a little."

"Whenever he passed out, we tied him up good, run his horse off, and left him out there to crawl home."

They all laughed again, a hearty laugh.

"What the hell did you do that for?" said Carl George.

The cowhands' faces fell. The question was totally unexpected. They were looking for praise, not chastisement.

"Well, why not?" asked one.

"He works with them Newmans," said another. "He couldn't a been up to no good."

"You should have brought him on in to the ranch house so we could find out what he wanted," Carl George said. "Now you've likely started a fight with the Newmans."

"We can handle that, can't we?"

"Never mind, Carl George," said Crowe. "They did right. He shouldn't have been on my place. I ain't starting no range war, but if they start it, we'll finish it, and we'll come out ahead on the deal."

Carl George stood up and stared down the lane that led out to the main road. He saw a buggy coming. "We got visitors," he said.

"Who is it?" said Crowe.

"I can't tell yet," said Carl George. "They're in a buggy."

Crowe stood up and walked to the top of the stairs that led up to the porch. Carl George and the other cowboys all stood on each side of him, forming a straight line. They stood there and waited 'til the buggy rolled up and came to a stop.

"Hello, Ernie," said Carl George. "Who's that you got with you?"

"This here is Mr. Slick Hannah from St. Looey," said Ernie, "and this is his, uh, his man, Ziggie. I brought them out here on account of they wanted to have a talk with you."

Not waiting for an invitation, Slick and Ziggie both

climbed down out of the buggy. Ziggie stood to one side, but Slick mounted the stairs and held out his right hand, a broad smile on his face.

"Mr. Crowe?" he said.

"I'm Crowe," Crowe responded, not putting out his hand. Slick dropped his hand to his side. "What do you want with me?"

"A little cooperation," Slick said. "That's all. Can we sit down someplace and talk?"

"We can talk here," Crowe said.

Ernie thought that he should say something about the body in the road, but he was afraid to interrupt Slick, so he kept it to himself. Slick apparently did not think it important enough to mention.

"Well, now, Mr. Crowe," Slick said, "what I got to talk to you about is kind a private, you know?"

"We can talk in front of all these men," Crowe said. "They work for me. We have no secrets."

"All right then," said Slick. He was uncomfortable standing in the yard at the foot of the stairs looking up at Crowe, but Crowe made no move to step aside and invite him up on the porch. "I want you and your boys to join up with my men to do a job."

"Why should I want to do that?"

"I understand that the Newmans, your neighbors over here, is your enemies."

"I have lots of enemies. Any man who gets as rich and powerful as I have makes enemies. So what?"

"Together we could wipe them out," Slick said. "It ain't just me and Ziggie here. I got six more boys back in town. And we got Black and Ernie here, and whoever else Black can round up. We could take them easy with you and your boys along."

"I have no reason to attack my neighbors, Mr.—

"Hannah. Slick Hannah."

"I have no reason to attack my neighbors, Mr. Hannah. What reason do you have?"

"They got something that I want," said Slick. "What do you say?"

"I say no."

"Are you scared? I heard you stole some land off of 'em. They'll just be waiting their chance to get even with you for that. Why not get them first?"

"Mr. Hannah, is it? I don't appreciate your coming to my house uninvited and accusing me of wrongdoing. This discussion is over. Ernie, you can drive these men back to town."

"Now, listen here," Slick started to say, but he shut his mouth when all the cowhands on the porch pulled out their six-guns and thumbed back the hammers. He and Ziggie were back in the buggy in no time. Ernie tipped his hat nervously.

"Uh, see you around, Mr. Crowe," he said.

Slocum rode slowly up to the Newman ranch house. His head was hanging so he did not notice Aubrey Newman at the corral. Aubrey saw him though and came running. He reached up to help Slocum out of the saddle.

"Slocum," he said. "What the hell happened to you?"

"Get these goddamned ropes off me, Aubrey," Slocum said, "and get someone to take care of my horse, will you?"

"Sure. Sure," Aubrey said, as he busied himself with the ropes. "Bartley," he called out. Bartley came out of the barn looking curious. He saw what Aubrey was doing and came running.

"Bartley," said Aubrey, "take care of Slocum's horse."

"What happened?" Bartley asked.

"We'll find out in good time," Aubrey said. "Right now, just take care of the horse."

"Don't kill Bartley, horse," Slocum said. "He's a friend."

Bartley took the reins and led the Appaloosa toward the corral. Aubrey finished getting the ropes off Slocum and led him up to a chair on the porch. Slocum sat down heavily.

"You want to tell me what happened now?" Aubrey said.

"I'd sure like to have a glass of whiskey," said Slocum.

"All right," said Aubrey. "Sure thing. I'll be right back. Don't go nowhere."

Aubrey disappeared into the house. When he returned a moment later, he was followed by Hiram, Maudie, Silly Sally, and Agnes. About that same time, Bartley came running back from the corral. Aubrey handed Slocum the glass of whiskey, and Slocum took a long drink. Everyone was crowded around him waiting for the story.

16

Calvin Black made it to Baxter Springs. He had worn out his horse, so he sold it cheap to the man in the livery. He got himself a room in a hotel and went to the nearest saloon to get himself a few drinks. Then he retired to his room to think about his situation. He knew that he had to stay away from Coffeyville for a time. He had to give the Hannah gang enough time to get its job done and get the hell out of there. Only when that was done would he go back. He figured that now that he had run out on Hannah, Hannah would kill him or have him killed if he ever saw him again.

He had left in such a hurry though, on the spur of the moment, so to speak, that he did not have much money on him. Oh, he had more on him than most people carried around with them, but he was going to have to live on it for a time. Baxter Springs was close enough to Coffeyville, though, that he could probably get the bank to contact his bank and get him some more money. He decided that he would do that right away.

The other situation he was facing was that, if the Hannah gang got its job done, they would be passing through Baxter Springs on their way back to St. Louis, and, of course, Black had no way of knowing when that time would come. He decided that he could get copies of the stage and train schedules. When it was time for either a stage or a train to be coming through town, he would stay in his hotel room and peek out the window to see if they came in, and he would keep watching to make sure they left again on the next transportation out of town.

He did not think that Slick and his boys would be coming through too soon, so he walked to the bank to take care of that important business. There was no problem, except that it would take a few days to get the deal taken care of. Well, he had enough cash on him to handle that. He walked back to the saloon and went inside. The saloon girls had shown up for work by then.

Black stopped at the bar and ordered himself another drink. While he was sipping it, a youngish woman walked up to him with a wide smile plastered across her face. "Buy a gal a drink?" she said.

"I'll go you one better than that," Black said. "I'll get a bottle and two glasses, and we can head over to the hotel to my room. What do you say to that?"

"Ooh," she said. "I could go for that."

They had stretched Slocum out on a bed in the ranch house and practically stripped his clothes off. He had three women messing around on him fixing him up. The men were lurking around the room back out of the way. Slocum had told the whole tale of what had happened to him out there on the range.

"What did you want to talk to old Crowe for anyway?" Hiram asked.

"Oh, hell," said Slocum. "I don't know. I guess I just wanted to try to figure out where he stands, to see if we're going to have to worry about him in the deal."

"I think we can count on Crowe to stay away from anything that looks like trouble," Aubrey said. "That's the reason he got Thornton to handle his dirty work in the first place."

"What are we going to do about those damn Crowe hands?" said Bartley.

"What do you mean?" Aubrey asked.

"We ain't going to just let them get away with beating up on Slocum like that, are we?"

"Don't worry about it," said Slocum. He winced as Maudie daubed something on his face. "I've been dealt a whole lot worse than this."

Hiram laughed. "I'll say. I remember a few of those times."

"That ain't the point," Bartley said. "We just can't let them get away with it. That's all."

"Bartley," said Slocum. "Ow, Maudie, that hurt."

"So you can take it, can't you, you big strong man?"

"That's worse than taking a beating," Slocum said. "Bartley, what happened today is between me and those boys. If I ever see them again, they'll pay the price."

"One thing occurs to me," said Aubrey. "Bartley might be right. What they did to you might be an indication of what's to come."

"I see what you mean," Hiram said. "Maybe when those ole boys jumped you like that, Slocum, they was announcing that Crowe's declaring war on us."

"I reckon that's a possibility," Slocum said, "but don't react to it just yet. Let's hold off a little while and see what happens next. You still got your guard out?"

"Damn right," Aubrey said.

"Well, put another one out," Slocum said, "over by that new fence line."

Slick Hannah alternately fumed and sulked on the ride all the way back into town. "I don't let people talk to me like that," he said.

"And run us off with guns," said Ziggie.

"The son of a bitch is going to have to pay," Slick said. "After I get that gal, I'll take care of that fucking Crowe."

"And his rube cowboys," Ziggie added.

"I'll teach him he can't talk to me like that. He can't treat me like I'm a nobody. I'm a big man. Everybody in St. Louis knows who I am."

Ernie thought, You're a long ways out of St. Looey, but he kept his thought to himself. It just did not seem like the right time to voice such a thought. He wondered where the hell his boss was hiding out. Hiding out. That was it. Black had run away from these city bastards and was hiding out somewhere waiting for them to clear out and go back to St. Looey. Then, he would be back. In the meantime, Ernie would just have to deal with them himself, or run out of town himself. He didn't have the money for that though. Then it came to him that with Calvin Black out of town, he did have complete control over the money that was coming into the saloon, even the gal money. He could hang on to everything he took in for the next couple of days, and then he would have enough to clear out on. That thought gave him a good deal of comfort.

The thought of the gal money brought something else to his mind. He had not seen Silly Sally for some time. She was a good moneymaker. She could almost always get a man to buy her a drink, and the drinks that men bought for her in the saloon were usually just colored water. Only if a man bought a bottle and got a couple of glasses and sat down with her at a table where he poured the drinks did she drink real whiskey. Or if a man took her to a room and took a bottle along. But if the man just bought her one drink at a time, Ernie always faked it. Of course, he charged the man the full price of a shot or a glass of whiskey. He wondered what the hell had become of Silly Sally.

"Are we about to get back to town?" Ziggie asked.

"We still got a few miles to go," said Ernie. "We ain't gone past the Newman ranch yet."

"Oh, yeah," said Ziggie.

"I don't like what's been going on around here," said Slick. "The sheriff went and got himself killed, your boss has disappeared. Maybe he's laying out beside a road somewhere. Who the hell is killing them?"

"I sure don't know," said Ernie.

"I just want to get my business done and get the hell out of here," Slick said.

Black took the saloon gal by her arm and started to lead her out of the place. As they walked toward the door, the barkeep looked up at them. She turned her head and gave him a wink. Then they walked out the door.

"What's your name?" Black asked.

"Melvina," she said.

"Melvina," said Black. "That's okay. Do you sing?"

"No. I can't carry a tune."

"We'll see."

They walked on into the hotel and past the desk, where the clerk gave a knowing look and went on about his business. Black took Melvina up the stairs. They walked a short distance down the hallway, and he stopped and unlocked a door. Pushing the door open, he stepped aside to allow Melvina to go in first. Then he followed, shut, and locked the door. He went to the bed and sat down, putting the two glasses on the bedside table, uncorking the bottle and pouring both glasses full. Melvina gave him a questioning look.

"Undress," he said.

She started stripping off her clothes to reveal a still fine-looking body. When she was naked, Black picked up a glass and held it out toward her. She walked over to him and took the glass, taking a healthy drink before she put it back on the table.

"Sing me a song," said Black.

"I don't know any songs," Melvina said, "and even if I did, like I told you, I can't carry a tune. I couldn't carry a tune in a bucket."

She laughed nervously.

"Sing," said Black.

Melvina thought for a moment, scratching her head, and at last the lyrics of a song came to her. She started to sing and dance a little while she sang. Black burst into laughter. She stopped singing and stood still, a serious pout on her face. Finally, Black stopped laughing. He wiped his eyes and took a deep breath.

"That wasn't very nice," Melvina said.

"Ah, never mind about that," said Black. "It was just good, clean fun. That's all." He picked up his glass and took a long drink. Putting the glass back down, he stood up and took off his coat. Melvina hurried over to take the coat. She hung it on a hook on the wall and went back to him.

"Can I help you?" she said.

"Yeah," said Black.

Melvina took off his shirt and hung it up. Then she knelt in front of him and pulled off his boots, placing them neatly beside the table. His trousers came off next, and he was standing in his long underwear. Soon Melvina had him out of that. He pulled her to him and held her close in their nakedness, reaching his arms around her to squeeze her round buttocks. She raised her head to look in his face. He gazed into her eyes for a moment, and then he said, "Get in bed."

Melvina pulled the covers down and crawled in. Black stood for a moment looking down at her, as she let her legs fall apart to reveal her waiting love hole. He reached down to take hold of his dong, and he stroked it a few times until it stood out stiff and hard. Then he crawled in on top of her. He poked his prick toward her hole, jabbing two or three times without success.

"Get it in there," he said.

Melvina reached down with both hands and took hold of Black's throbbing cock. She guided it into her waiting, wet hole and thrust upward with her pelvis. At the same time, Black shoved as hard as he could, driving his full length into her waiting, hungry cunt. Both of them started humping furiously, moaning out loud, and gasping for breath. They were like two alley cats, desperate in heat.

Finally, Black stopped thrusting and rested for a moment, his cock still hard, still deep in her pussy. Then he withdrew and put his hands on her hips, turning her over on her stomach. He pulled her up onto her knees and drove his cock into her again from behind. He banged into her so hard that her whole body shook with each thrust, her ass wriggling in time with him. Tiring again from so much work, Black pulled out and lay back, his rod sticking straight up. Melvina straddled him and mounted him like she was mounting a wild stallion, sitting on the hard tool and letting it slide all the way in again.

Then she started to rock back and forth, sliding along on his wet belly. He just lay still enjoying the sensation, moaning with pleasure, nearly exhausted, breathing deeply. "Oh, oh," he moaned.

"Yes, yes," she said.

Black reached both hands around to grab her ass, one cheek in each hand as she continued rocking. All of a sudden, he slapped one cheek, hard. "Oh," she cried, rocking even faster. He slapped the other cheek, and he continued slapping alternately, one hand and then the other. She kept crying out, "Oh, oh," and kept rocking. At last Black felt the powerful surge building deep inside. He began thrusting upward as she continued rocking until the first salvo shot forth. Then another and another. Finally he lay still, panting, and she fell forward to lay on his chest. His cock grew soft and limp inside her. Then it slipped out.

Black shoved her off of him to one side. He rolled over and reached for the glasses on the table. Handing her one glass, he took the other. They each had a sip of whiskey. "Stick around, Mel," he said. "We might just have another go."

17

The buggy came to the entrance to the Newman ranch, and Slick told Ernie to stop. Ernie hauled back on the reins. The buggy rocked to a halt. Slick got down and stood in the road studying the place.

"What are you doing, boss?" Ziggie asked.

"We're going to have to take this place by ourselves," said Slick. "The sheriff's dead, Black's disappeared, and old man Crowe ain't going to be no help. I'm just looking over the lay of the land."

"You can barely see the house from here," said Ziggie.

"Maybe we'll sneak in a little closer," said Slick. "Get a better look."

"You want me to do that?"

"Yeah. Go on ahead."

Finis Newman was standing guard, hidden in some brush. He saw the buggy stop in the road, saw that Ernie was driving it, saw the passengers. He watched as the one man moved toward the gate.

Ziggie halted at the gate and looked toward the house. He scouted around some more, studying places of concealment, trying to figure out a safe approach to the house. He could see the hay bales stacked around the house and placed strategically in the yard.

"What are you waiting for?" Slick said.

Ziggie reached under his coat and pulled out a revolver. Then he moved forward, keeping to one side of the lane. Finis stood up, drawing his six-gun.

"Hey," he called out. "What are you doing here."

Ziggie spun toward the sound and fired a round. The bullet caught Finis in the chest. He looked surprised. His hand went limp, and he dropped his gun. Then his face went blank, and he fell backward. Ziggie turned and ran back to the buggy.

"Let's get the hell out of here," he said.

Ernie and Slick piled back in as fast as they could, and Ziggie was only about halfway in when Ernie lashed out at the horse. The buggy lurched forward, and Ziggie toppled into the dirt. He landed hard, knocking the wind out of his lungs. He tried to shout out for them to stop, but he could not get any air.

"Hey," said Slick, "you dropped Ziggie. Hold it up."

Ernie stopped the buggy and looked at Slick.

"They'll be coming out from the house any time," he said. "They had to hear the shot."

Slick was already out of the buggy.

"Shut up," he said. "Wait here."

He ran back to help Ziggie. Ernie panicked. He whipped up the horse again and raced down the road. Slick turned to see him going.

"God damn it," he called out. "Get back here. You son of a bitch."

The buggy raced on. Slick pulled out his gun and

pointed it at the fleeing buggy, but then he realized that his shot would be wild. The buggy had already gotten too far away. He hurried back to Ziggie who was at last sucking in deep breaths of air.

"Ziggie," he said, "you all right?"

"Yeh," said Ziggie. "Had the wind knocked out of me."

Slick gave him a hand and helped him to his feet.

"What'd you do back there?"

"I shot a guy."

Slick looked up and down the road in desperation. Opposite the gateway to the Newman ranch was thick woods. The buggy was long gone.

"Come on," he said. He led Ziggie into the woods and into deep tangles of brush. Wild rosebush caught them in its thorns and pulled at their clothes.

"God damn," said Ziggie.

"Shut up and keep moving," said Slick.

Just then the merciless brambles reached around Slick's ankles, grabbing tightly and Slick fell forward, landing hard on the ground.

"God damn it," he said. "Ziggie, help me outa here."

Ziggie looked back over his shoulder. He saw no one coming after them. He reached into his pocket and pulled out a penknife and began slashing at the brambles that held Slick down.

"Hurry up, Ziggie. Hurry up," said Slick, impatiently.

"I'm getting them, boss. I'm getting them. Ouch."

At last Ziggie had cut Slick free. His hands were sliced up by the thorns. He grabbed Slick by a coat sleeve and pulled him to his feet. Slick started moving deeper into the woods.

• • •

Slocum was dressed again and sitting on the porch with Aubrey. His face showed bruises and cuts, but he was all right. He was having a cup of coffee and smoking a cigar when they heard the shot.

"That came from the gate," said Aubrey.

They put down their cups and hurried off the porch. As they continued running toward the road, they were joined by Finis's brother George. Getting closer to the gate, each man pulled out his revolver. They had no idea what they would encounter at the gate. Closer yet, they slowed down, looking all around as they made their final approach. Slocum was the first to the gate. He looked up and down the road, but he saw nothing. Aubrey joined him there. George was looking around inside the gate, looking toward the places where Finis might have secreted himself.

"Something's wrong, Slocum," Aubrey said. "Finis was out here."

"Yeah," Slocum said. "Let's look for him. There's no one out here."

They turned to walk back in and look around, but they saw George standing stock-still, his head hanging, his arms dangling limply at his sides.

"George?" said Aubrey.

Slocum and Aubrey hurried over to his side, and then they saw what George had found. Finis was there on the ground—dead.

Ziggie and Slick finally stopped running and sat down on the ground to lean back against the trunks of trees. They were panting and trying to catch their breath.

"Boss?" said Ziggie between his gasps.

"What?"

"What are we going to do?"

"We're going to walk back to town," said Slick. "What else? Unless you know how to fly."

"Do you know where we are?"

"Sure I know," said Slick. "We're just in the woods off to the side of the road there by the god damn Newman ranch. That's where we are."

"Which way's the road?"

"It's just off that way," said Slick, pointing. He hesitated. "No. A little more over there. That's the way."

"I hope you're sure about that," Ziggie said.

"Look," said Slick, "we can't go back out that way anyhow. Those cowboys will be out looking to see if they can find who it was that shot their pal. How come you went and shot him anyhow?"

"I didn't have no choice, boss," Ziggie said. "He had a gun."

"All right. All right. Forget about it. We're just going to have to take a long hike. That's all."

Aubrey and George had taken the body back to the house. Slocum stayed behind to study the road. He found buggy tracks, and it looked to him like the buggy had stopped, then raced ahead. He couldn't be sure, but he strongly suspected that someone in a buggy had been there and done the shooting. The question now was, Who would be out in a buggy? Cowhands from the Crowe ranch would be on horseback. He thought about the gangsters from St. Louis. He walked back to the corral and saddled his Appaloosa. Aubrey caught up with him.

"Where you going, Slocum?" he asked.

"Heading into town," Slocum said. "Someone was out there in a buggy."

"I'm going with you."

Aubrey was soon saddled up, and the two rode into Coffeyville. They followed the buggy tracks all the way in. They wound up at the livery stable. Aubrey called the liveryman out.

"What can I do for you?" the man said.

"Who brought that buggy back in here?" said Slocum.

"Why, it was Ernie, Calvin Black's barkeep."

"Thanks," Slocum said, starting to turn his horse.

"Funny thing though," said the liveryman.

Slocum turned back.

"What's funny?" Aubrey asked.

"When he drove out earlier, he had two of them city slickers with him. He come back alone."

Aubrey and Slocum exchanged looks of curiosity. They turned their horses and rode to the saloon. It was locked.

"Do you know where Ernie lives?" Slocum asked.

Ernie was already headed out of town on horseback. He had collected all the cash he had been taking in at the saloon, every penny, and he had started out again when he saw Slocum and Aubrey riding into town. He had ducked back inside the saloon, locked the door and gone out the back way. In the alley, he saw a saddled horse standing behind the saddle shop. Desperate to get away, he mounted the horse and rode out. Without any planning, he was headed for Baxter Springs. He lashed at the horse, riding viciously.

• • •

"Far as I know," Aubrey said, "Ernie's got a room over the saloon."

"Let's check the back door," Slocum said.

They rode around to the back and found the door there not only unlocked but standing open. Securing their mounts, they went inside. The six gangsters were sitting at a table in the saloon, and a couple of the saloon gals were standing on the landing at the top of the stairs.

"What's going on?" said one the girls.

"We're looking for Ernie," said Slocum.

"You seen him?" said Aubrey.

"We seen him all right," said one gal.

"He come in here real fast," said the other. "He come up here to his room, and when we spoke to him, he didn't even answer."

"He went in his room and come right back out, tucking something in his pocket, and he run out the back door. Why ain't we open?"

"Where's Black and where's Ernie gone?"

"That's what we'd like to know," Aubrey said.

"Ernie left outa here with our boss and Ziggie," one of the gangsters volunteered. "I'd like to know where's the boss and Ziggie."

"If we find them, we'll let you know," Slocum said.

Slocum and Aubrey went back into the alley and mounted their horses.

"What now?" Aubrey asked.

"I ain't sure," said Slocum, "but Ernie's not far away."

They started to ride down the alley, and a couple of the gangsters had walked to the back door where they stood staring out at them. Just then a man came out the back door of the saddle shop. He stopped, looking astonished, then angry. He looked up at Slocum and Aubrey who were riding in his direction.

"You see anyone else in this alley?" he asked.

"No, we ain't," said Aubrey.

"God damn it," the man said. "Some son of a bitch has stole my horse."

Slocum studied the ground and saw where the horse had gone. It had been moving fast.

"He was in a hurry," Slocum said. "If we find him, we'll get him back to you."

As Slocum and Aubrey headed out after the horse, and hopefully after Ernie, the man shouted after them, "Don't shoot the bastard. Bring him back here to hang."

The horse thief had been moving fast and so did the two riding in pursuit. When they got out of town, Slocum's Appaloosa easily outdistanced the cow pony that Aubrey was riding. Slocum rode hard for a couple of miles, then slowed down. Aubrey caught up with him and slowed his cow pony.

"No sign of him yet," Aubrey said.

"We'll catch him," said Slocum. "If he ain't slowed his pace yet, he'll kill the horse. One way or another, we'll catch up with him."

"So, if Ernie drove out of town with two of those gangsters, and then come back to town without them, what the hell happened to them?" Aubrey asked.

"That's the Big Question, Aubrey," Slocum said. "If we can catch him without killing him, we'll ask him."

18

Slick and Ziggie had to sit down and rest once more. Although Slick was hesitant to admit to it, he was hopelessly lost, turned around completely in the deep woods. He did not know the direction back to the road, the direction back to town, or the direction to any kind of civilization anywhere. He was desperate to get back to town and organize his gang to hit the Newman place and get rid of the Glitch woman and any other witnesses out here in the goddamned Wild West to anything that he had done. That now included Ernie. He had to find Ernie and get rid of him because Ernie had witnessed Ziggie's killing of that cowboy, and because Ernie had run out on them and left them in this goddamned mess. Slick was itching to find Ernie and kill him.

On the other hand, Ziggie was just itching. He wondered what he had gotten into that was causing him to itch so badly. He was scratching his legs and his arms, the backs of his hands, and something was tormenting him terribly between the toes of his right foot. He also wanted a drink in the worst way. He wanted to be back in town, in the hotel room, sitting in a hot bath with a drink in his hand. He wasn't thinking of his boss's problems, of the Glitch woman, or of Ernie, or of anyone else. He was itching like hell.

"Boss," he said, "we got to figure out how to get out of this fucking jungle."

"I know that, Ziggie. You think I don't know that? Just look at me. My suit is all torn up. I'm scratched all over. I'm hungry and I want a drink. You think I don't know we gotta get outa here? Shit. God damn."

"I'm itching like fire all over me," Ziggie said. "Damn. It just got to my balls."

"Come on," said Slick. "Let's get going."

"Where?"

"I don't know where, but we gotta do something. We can't just sit here."

"Why not? If we get going and we go in the wrong direction, we'll just be that much farther off from where we need to be. What's the sense in going if we don't know where we're going?"

"Ziggie, any direction we go has got to lead us somewhere. And anywhere we get to has got to be better than this. Come on now."

Slocum rounded a bend in the road and saw a rider up ahead. He slowed his pace, and again, Aubrey caught up with him. "Is that Ernie?" Aubrey asked.

"I can't tell yet," Slocum said, "but I'd just about bet on it. Let's catch up with him, but not too fast."

They picked up their pace a little, slowly closing the gap between themselves and the other rider. They rode like that for perhaps another mile, when suddenly the other rider, apparently just then aware that he was being followed, turned his head to look over his shoulder. He spotted them, then turned back forward and lashed at his horse.

"It's him," Slocum said. "Let's get him."

The Appaloosa was closing the gap quickly, and Aubrey and his horse were not far behind. Ernie, for indeed it was Ernie, pulled out a gun and turned in the saddle to fire. His shot was wild. He kept riding ahead. He fired again. Again it was wild. He raced around a curve, and Slocum lost sight of him for the moment. Moving on around the curve, Slocum could not see Ernie anywhere ahead, and the road was straight for a while. He pulled up his Appaloosa quickly. He backed up. Aubrey caught up and reined in beside him.

"What happened?" he said.

"I lost him around that bend," Slocum said. "He's off the side of the road. No way he could be that far ahead."

Lurking behind a bush, his horse a little farther back in the woods, Ernie held his gun ready. All he had was a revolver. He knew he could not afford to take any risky long shots. If they thought they had lost him, maybe they would turn around and go back. But if they came closer, he would shoot. He was no gunfighter, but he was a fairly good shot, and he could drop them, one at a time, he knew, if they rode close enough and did not spot him along the way. He hunkered down farther, hoping to stay out of sight.

"Let's walk," said Slocum, and he and Aubrey dismounted and tied their horses at the side of the road. They began walking slowly ahead, watching on both sides as they moved. A horse nickered not too far distant. Slocum turned toward the sound, and a shot rang out. He and Aubrey ran to the sides of the road.

"Slocum," Aubrey called out.

Slocum looked in his direction from the other side of the road. Aubrey motioned to a place not too far ahead of Slocum and on Slocum's side.

"He's over there."

Slocum nodded. He started inching closer. Aubrey, on the other hand, suddenly ran out into the middle of the road, and Ernie stood up to take a shot at him. Slocum saw him and stood and fired just as Ernie fired. Ernie's shot nicked Aubrey's shoulder, and Aubrey spun around at the impact. Slocum's caught Ernie in the chest. Ernie dropped out of sight. Slocum looked in Ernie's direction, then looked back at Aubrey. He ran to Aubrey and helped him to the side of the road.

"That was a damn fool move," he said.

"It worked, didn't it?" said Aubrey.

"You all right?"

"Yeah. Go get him."

Leaving Aubrey there, Slocum moved toward Ernie. He wasn't sure how badly Ernie had been hit, so he remained cautious. But Ernie did not reappear and did not shoot again. Slocum suddenly came on Ernie, lying back in the brush, his chest covered with blood, his revolver on the ground beside him. Slocum's Colt was pointed directly at Ernie. When he saw that he was safe, he holstered the Colt and knelt beside Ernie.

"You got me good," Ernie said.

"Did you steal that horse?" Slocum asked.

"Yeah, but that ain't the worst. I got what I deserve. I killed the preacher."

"Who killed the man back at the Newman ranch?"

"Ziggie."

"Who?"

"Slick Hannah's man, Ziggie. He killed him."

"Where are Slick and Ziggie?"

"I left them standing in the road by the Newman place. I ran off and left them. They were planning to attack—"

Ernie never finished his last sentence. He had breathed his last breath. He died, and Slocum went through his pockets. He found a bundle of cash, and he tucked it in his shirt. He picked up the revolver and stuck it in his waistband. Then he went a bit deeper into the woods and found the horse where Ernie had hidden it. He unloosed the reins and led it out to the road. Returning to Aubrey, Slocum said, "Ernie's done for. Let's get you back to the ranch."

"Town's closer," Aubrey said. "There's a doc in town."

"Okay."

They mounted up and headed back toward Coffeyville leading the stolen horse.

At the sound of the shots, Slick and Ziggie stopped moving. They looked at each other and then in the direction the shots had come from.

"Shots," said Ziggie.

"I heard them," said Slick. "They come from that way."

Slick started to move in the direction of the shots.

"Hey, boss," Ziggie said, "we don't want to walk into the middle of no gunfight."

"We got no choice," Slick said. "Come on."

They hurried through the woods, Ziggie scratching at his ass as they moved. Slick was in such a hurry that he stumbled and fell down twice. At last, though, they reached the edge of the woods. They were looking out on the road.

"We made it, Ziggie."

"I ain't sure this is the same road."

"There's only one road out here in the middle of this damn desert," said Slick. "This is the road, and there ain't no gunfight going on. Whatever it was, it's finished."

Ziggie scratched furiously at his balls. "So which direction is town?"

"It'll be that way," Slick said, pointing.

They started to walk. By this time, both men were miserable. Their legs were aching, and their feet were blistered. Their mouths were dry, and their throats were parched with thirst. They were hungry, and they were damned tired. They walked along a ways before Ziggie said, "Boss, I got to sit down for a minute."

"Okay," said Slick. They walked to the side of the road. Ziggie looked for a place to sit. He dropped to the ground and put out a hand and touched something that made him jump. He looked and saw Ernie's bloody body.

"Aah!" he screamed in surprise.

"What the hell?" said Slick. "What is it?"

Ziggie stood up and pointed. "Right here," he said. "Somebody beat us to it." He scratched his ass. "It's Ernie shot through the chest. He's dead as a mackerel."

Slick walked over to look. "Well, I'll be damned," he said. "I can't say I'm sorry, the little weasel. I'd a liked it better if I coulda done it myself." He spat on the body. "It's his fault, this mess we're in."

Ziggie spat on it too, and then he scratched his balls. "I got to take a piss," he said, and he hauled out his itching tool and relieved himself on the body of the unfortunate Ernie. A victim of the power of suggestion, Slick did the same thing. Tucking away his limp rod, Slick said, "Well, that's done. Let's get to hoofing it back to town."

• • •

Slocum and Aubrey made it back to town. Slocum left Aubrey with the doctor. Then he found the horse's owner and returned the horse. "I'm sorry," he said, "but there won't be no hanging."

"You had to kill the bastard?" the man asked.

"Afraid so," Slocum said.

"Did you know him?"

"It was Ernie, the barkeep."

"Well, I'll be damned."

Slocum then went back to the saloon where he called the girls down. He did not see the gangsters, but he figured they could be anywhere. The girls gathered around Slocum at the bar.

"Did you find Ernie?" one asked.

"I found him," Slocum said. "He won't be coming back."

He reached in his shirt and hauled out the bundle of money. They girls' eyes grew big and their mouths fell open. Slocum dropped the money on the bar.

"Black's vanished," he said. "Ernie's dead. I guess this money belongs to you all. I'm taking a share out for Silly Sally. You can divide up the rest."

As soon as Slocum left, the girls counted the money and split it up among them. Then one said, "Let's get out of here before those city dudes get back. I don't like them."

"I don't like them either," said another, "but where will we go?"

"Over to the hotel for now," said the first one. "We got the cash."

And with that, they all rushed out of the saloon.

• • •

Slocum went back to the doctor's office for Aubrey and found him all patched up. "It's not bad," said the doc. "He was lucky."

Aubrey paid the doctor and left with Slocum.

"I guess those two ain't come back to town yet," he said.

"Nope," said Slocum. "According to Ernie's last words, they're likely out there somewhere trying to find their way back on foot."

"Do we wait for them?"

"I'd rather get you home."

"Aw, hell, I'm all right."

"I'd rather get you home."

"I heard you the first time," Aubrey said. "All right. Let's go."

They mounted their horses and rode toward the ranch.

Outside of town, Slick Hannah and Ziggie were still trudging alone, each step of each man a horror of pain.

"Ziggie," said Slick, "when we get back I'm going to the room. I'm going to order up a bath."

"Two baths," said Ziggie.

"I'm going to order us up two baths and two bottles of whiskey and two big steak dinners. I'm going to tell them to keep pouring hot water in the tubs all night long, and if one of the bottles gets empty, I'm calling for another."

"We'll get drunk as two skunks," said Ziggie, as he limped along the road and scratched at his ass.

19

Carl George knocked on the front door of the big house, and from inside, old man Crowe yelled out, "Come on in." Carl George opened the door, took off his hat, stepped inside, and closed the door behind him.

"You got a minute, Mr. Crowe?"

"Come on in and sit down, Carl George," said Crowe.

Carl George sat down. Crowe took a seat just opposite him. "What's on your mind?" he said.

"Mr. Crowe, I been doing a lot of thinking."

"That can be dangerous, Carl George, too much thinking."

"Yeah. I know."

"Well, go on. What you been thinking about?"

"Sooner or later, there's going to be a range war here."

"You mean, us and them Newmans?"

"Yes, sir. That's my meaning."

"Go on,"

"And there's them city dudes. I sure don't like the look that one give you whenever you run them off. I think he means to do something. To get even somehow. Men like him are like that. They don't just walk away whenever they've been insulted."

"You think I insulted him, Carl George?"

"I think he took it thataway."

"And you think he'll come back out here and try to do something to get even with me. Is that it?"

"Yes, sir. That's what I been thinking. There's eight of them all together, and he said that he had Ernie and some other boys in with them."

"That could be quite a crowd to do battle with."

"It could."

"So what are you thinking we ought to do?"

"I'm thinking that we ought to go ahead and attack the Newmans. Get that over with and done."

"Wipe them out?"

"To the last man."

"And woman?"

Carl George paused for a moment, and then he said, "And woman."

Crowe sat silent for a moment. He sipped from his whiskey glass. "All right, Carl George," he said. "We'll do it. At dawn tomorrow morning."

"There's one thing we need to do first, Mr. Crowe," Carl George said.

"What's that?"

"They've got a man posted over there just the other side of our new fence line to watch. I'd say he was watching for us to make some kind of move toward them."

"Send a man out there tonight to take care of him," said Crowe.

• • •

Slick and Ziggie stumbled up to the saloon door. It was open by this time, for the other six gang members had opened it when they went out. They were back though, and Slick and Ziggie found them sitting around a table drinking. Slick and Ziggie wobbled their way to the table. They fell into chairs. Ziggie scratched his balls.

"Give us a bottle," said Slick.

One of the men shoved a bottle toward Slick who grabbed it up and drank from it. He passed it on to Ziggie. While Ziggie was chugging from the bottle, Slick said, "Go get another bottle and a couple of glasses."

A gangster went to the bar and returned with them. Slick poured a couple of drinks. Finally one of the men got up enough courage to ask, "What happened to you two?"

"Never mind that," Slick said. "Have someone fix us a couple of baths up in the rooms."

"There ain't no one here, boss," said the man.

"No one?"

"No one. Even the gals is gone."

"Go over to the hotel and get us a room. Have them fix two baths in it. Tell them to hurry it up."

The gangster hurried out of the saloon. Slick turned to another one. You take a couple of bottles and a couple of glasses over there."

The man rushed to do what he'd been told to do. Then Slick turned to a third one. "Go to the restaurant and order up two steak dinners. Have them delivered to the hotel room."

That man rushed out. Slick took another drink.

"What happened to everyone, boss?" asked one of the three men left at the table.

"Ernie's dead out on the road," Slick said. "We never found Black. Don't know what become of him."

"The gals all left sometime. I guess when we was out or when we went up to our rooms. Sometime."

"That don't matter," said Slick. "We'll be leaving ourselves before long now."

"Man," said one, "I'm sure ready."

"Are we moving to the hotel, boss?" asked another one.

"No," said Slick. "We're staying here on account of it don't cost us nothing. Me and Ziggie, we're going to a hotel room so we can get a bath. You go upstairs to our room and gather up clean clothes for the both of us. Take them over to the hotel room."

The man jumped up and hurried off, leaving Slick and Ziggie with two men at the table. Slick emptied his glass and poured another drink. Ziggie scratched his balls.

Slocum and Aubrey were sitting on the porch with Agnes and Silly Sally chewing the fat. Maudie was in the kitchen as usual, and Hiram had gone into town on banking business. Bartley started walking toward the house from the barn. He was carrying something in his hand, a short stick of some kind. When he came closer, he held it up over his head.

"Hey," he called out, "look what I found."

They all turned toward him, and when he got a little closer, he tossed the stick. Slocum caught it. It was a stick of dynamite.

"God damn," Slocum said.

"I'd forgot about that," said Hiram.

"Where'd it come from?" Slocum asked.

"We had it whenever we was getting some stumps out of the ground over in the south pasture," Aubrey said.

"That's dangerous stuff to leave lying around," said Slocum.

Bartley mounted the stairs, and Slocum held the stick out to him. Bartley took it.

"Yeah," he said. "It could be pretty dangerous to anyone who comes riding in here uninvited."

Slocum's eyes lit up. "Yeah," he said. "It sure could."

Slick and Ziggie sat in two tubs in the hotel room. Each had a bottle of whiskey in his hand. They had already eaten their steak dinners. Ziggie was still scratching, but at least it felt a little better underneath the warm sudsy water. Both men were getting drunk.

"I been thinking, Ziggie," said Slick.

"What about?"

"I been thinking that it's time we got the hell out of this damn one-horse town."

"I'm sure with you on that," Ziggie said.

"But we got a job to do first."

"Yeah?"

"We got to get that gal."

"Yeah," said Ziggie, his voice dropping low in disappointment. "How we going to do that?"

"We're going to rush that ranch house," Slick said. "There's eight of us. We can take it. There's nothing out there but a bunch of rubes. You got rid of one of them already."

"Yeah, but—"

"We'll rent us a wagon so we can all load up in it, and we'll drive out there and catch them by surprise."

"Who'll drive?" Ziggie asked.

"Hell, anyone. I can drive a fucking wagon. There ain't nothing to it. You just flick the reins and get it going. That's all."

Ziggie thought better of it, but he didn't argue. "When?" he asked.

"You and me got to get a good rest after what we been through," Slick said. "When we've had our rest, we'll call everyone together and talk about it."

Hiram was in the bank just having finished his business. He was about to turn and leave when the clerk said, "Say, Mr. Newman, do you know what's going on over at the saloon?"

"No. I don't go there. Why do you ask?"

"I heard today that there's no one there. The place is all closed down. And I got a request today from the bank over at Baxter Springs for a sizable transfer of cash from Calvin Black's account."

Hiram shrugged. "I don't have any idea," he said, and he left the bank.

On his way out of town, he noticed that the bank clerk had been right. The saloon was not open. He wondered what Calvin Black was up to in Baxter Springs. He already knew that Slocum had killed Ernie. There wasn't anyone else to run the place. He thought that Calvin's business had been pretty good, and it did not make sense for Calvin to just abandon the place and leave it to ruin. He knew that Slocum and Aubrey and the boys would be interested in this news.

Joseph Croy was sitting in his saddle near the new fence. He was watching the range on the other side, the range now claimed by old man Crowe. It was a boring job. He had not even seen any cattle since his turn came to watch. He hadn't seen any cowhands either. He rolled a smoke and lit it and was wishing that he was in town in the saloon having a drink or two and maybe a conversation with one of the gals. He told himself, trying to fight off the boredom, that Slocum was probably right, that someone needed to be doing this job in case the Crowe riders decided to make a move, but he wished that his time would hurry up and pass and he would be relieved.

Hell, let his brother Isaac sit out here and do nothing. Isaac didn't drink much, and he never messed with the saloon gals. He always thought that he was saving himself for the woman he would one day marry. He had not met that woman yet though, but he remained hopeful. Joseph liked to tease him about that.

"Have you ever heard that old saying, 'If you don't use it, you'll lose it'?" he would say to his brother.

"Cut it out, Joe," Isaac would say. "You're liable to catch some awful sickness the way you behave."

"If I do, I'll die happy," Joseph would answer.

"Mama wouldn't approve of the way you live," Isaac would say, and Joseph would answer, "What Mama don't know won't hurt her none."

The sun was getting low in the sky, and Joseph was squinting to see much of anything over toward the Crowe ranch headquarters. He didn't think it was very important, but he tried to watch anyway. It was his job. He guessed someone had to do it, so it might as well be him. He took a last drag on his cigarette and tossed it aside.

Off in the distance, on the other side of the fence, a lone rider was approaching. He moved slowly, riding at an angle, heading for a spot along the fence closer to the road, farther from where he thought the sentry would be waiting and watching. At last he reached the fence. He was right. There was no sentry in sight. He dismounted and lapped his reins around the top strand of wire. Then he slipped the rifle from the saddle boot, cranked a shell into the chamber, and stood looking around. There was no movement. He did not think he had been spotted. He walked slowly along the fence line.

Now and then he would kick a rock or step on a stick and make a noise, and then he would stop and watch and wait. There was no movement, no response to the noise he had made, so he would move on. Out at night like this, trying to move about undetected, any tiny noise was magnified a thousand times it seemed. He even thought that his breathing was loud. He tried to take fewer breaths, to wait longer between his breaths. He had an urge to cough, but he fought it back. Surely a sentry would hear a cough. He heard a horse nicker and stamp its feet, and he stopped. He looked ahead and spotted the huge shadowy figure. He waited until he could make it out better, a man sitting horseback. He raised the rifle to his shoulder, took careful aim, and squeezed the trigger. The man jerked in the saddle and the horse jumped nervously and took off running as the man fell off its back. The shooter ran closer to make sure that the sentry was dead. Then he turned around and hurried back to his own horse. Mounting up, he rode back a ways, paid out his rope, and lassoed one of the fence posts. He dismounted, walked to the fence, and cut all the wires. Then he remounted and rode hard, pulling down a section of fence. He threw the rope down on the ground and headed back toward the Crowe ranch headquarters.

20

Cousin George was supposed to relieve Joe Croy, but he got worried when he heard the faint sound of a rifle shot in the distance. He decided to ride out early to make sure that Joseph was all right. Joseph's brother, Isaac, heard George getting dressed. He sat up in his bed and looked bleary-eyed at George.

"Is it that time yet?" he said.

"Not yet," said George. "I think I heard a rifle shot. I'm going on out there to make sure everything's all right."

Isaac came fully awake and swung his legs off the side of his bed. He started pulling on his clothes.

"I'm going with you," he said.

"Ain't no need," said George.

"He's my brother."

They found Joseph lying dead near the fence line, his horse grazing nearby. George gave Isaac a few moments. He rode out a ways and looked around. When he went back to Isaac and the body, he said, "Isaac, why don't you take your brother on back. I'll stay here and keep watch."

Isaac loaded his brother's body on the back of the loose horse. He mounted his own horse, taking the reins of the other. As he turned the horses to head back, George said, "Tell them that the fence has been tore down. Sorry about your brother, Isaac."

When the Crowe bunch started riding, it was not quite daylight. The old man rode at the head, his cowhands riding in a wedge behind him. But for the lack of uniforms, they looked very like a small army setting out to do battle. Each man carried at least one six-gun and a rifle. They wore stern, somber faces and rode with determination. They were men with a purpose, and that purpose was hard. They rode toward the place where their man had torn down the fence.

When Isaac got back to the ranch house, he woke everyone up. He told them that his brother had been murdered and that George was out at the sentry post. He also told them the fence had been torn down. All of the Newman hands, including Slocum, dressed in a hurry and armed themselves. The three women made sure that guns were within reach in the house. Slocum stashed six sticks of dynamite in his saddlebags. They left four men at the house, and the rest mounted up and rode out toward the fence.

George saw the Crowe riders coming. He turned his horse and headed for the house. He had not gone far when he met the Newman riders on their way to the fence. "They're coming," he shouted. "The whole damn bunch."

"We're going to be outnumbered, boys," Hiram Newman shouted, "but let's give them hell."

Slocum put a cigar in his mouth and struck a match to light it. He puffed up clouds of smoke. Then he reached back into his saddlebag and pulled out a dynamite stick. "I mean to narrow those odds somewhat," he said.

They started riding to meet the foe, each man with a gun in his hand, each man except Slocum. When they saw the Crowe riders, it seemed that everyone started shooting. No one was hit. They were still too far apart for accuracy. On the other side of the fence was nothing but pasture, but on the Newman side there were trees.

"Dismount and take cover," Hiram shouted.

Everyone did so except Slocum. He rode ahead. When he thought the distance was just about right, he touched his cigar to the fuse. He held the stick for a moment while it fizzed. Then he dropped it right in the path of the oncoming riders. He turned his Appaloosa and rode back into the trees where he dismounted and ducked behind a tree like everyone else. The riders came on. Then, all of a sudden, there was a tremendous roar and a flash of light. Men and horses flew up in the air, and the air was filled with the acrid smell of burned powder and with flying dirt and debris.

The riders who were not hit all scattered in different directions. The explosion had taken out most of the right side of the wedge. Old man Crowe was just saved by a few feet. Men on both sides started firing, a few of the Newman shots finding their marks. The Crowe riders were firing wildly, not really knowing just where their targets were hidden. Old Crowe, realizing that he and his men were like sitting ducks in their saddles, shouted out orders to dismount. A couple of his men were slow to respond and were dropped from their saddles by Newman rifle shots. The rest got to the ground of their own volition. Most of them dropped to their bellies or down on one knee.

"Find your targets," shouted Carl George. "Don't waste bullets."

Watching for flashes of gunfire, the Crowe men at last discovered where the Newmans were hidden. The sun was just beginning to light up the sky, so the Crowe cowhands could see the Newmans when they showed themselves around the tree trunks to fire shots. But when the Crowe riders began firing, the Newmans simply disappeared behind their cover.

"Creep in closer," Crowe shouted.

As they crept, they came back together more. Slocum watched. He figured he could get another stick of dynamite among them. He crawled out from his cover in the trees until he was right close to the fence line. Then he touched his cigar to another fuse. He waited a bit while it fizzed. Then he stood up and ran closer. He flung the stick hard. He hit the ground and crawled back fast, and the explosion boomed out in the cool morning air. Slocum felt some of the dust falling on his back and he heard some screams. He stood up and ran back to the trees.

"God damn, Slocum," Hiram said. "You took out a few of them that time too."

"That's the idea," said Slocum.

"I seen three of them fly up into the air," said Aubrey.

"We got to rush them," said Crowe, out in the field.

"You heard the boss, men," said Carl George. "Let's go."

All of the remaining Crowe men stood at once and started to run at once. All of them were firing at the trees. The Newmans all ducked behind their trees to avoid the shots. Slocum lit another fuse and held it as long as he dared. He stepped out just long enough to toss the stick and ducked back behind the tree as a bullet smacked into the trunk. The blast took out four more Crowe men. This time, one of them was Carl George.

"Meet them head-on," Hiram Newman shouted, stepping out into the open with his six-gun blazing.

The rest of the Newmans stepped out and they all started walking toward the Crowe men. Both sides were firing. Men dropped on both sides. A bullet nicked Hiram Newman's left ear.

"By God," he shouted. He took aim and fired, and old Crowe fell dead, his face landing in a pile of fresh horse shit. Slocum threw yet another stick of dynamite. This last blast all but wiped out the Crowe riders. The last three men standing were gunned down easily by the Newmans. Finally all was quiet. The air was filled with the odor of blasted black powder. Horses nickered and stamped about nervously. Hiram and Slocum walked out on the corpse-strewn pasture to check on the dead. There was no one left alive out there.

"We wiped them plumb out," said Hiram.

"To the last man," said Slocum.

Hiram turned back toward his own men and shouted, "Aubrey, who have we lost?"

It was a minute before Aubrey responded. "Bartley's hurt. Not too bad. Isaac's dead."

Bartley was taken back to the ranch house to be patched up. Isaac's body was taken along to be buried beside his brother. Crowe and his men were buried where they had fallen.

Slocum took time out to rest and to contemplate the situation. One worry was behind them. The Crowe bunch was no longer a problem. He figured that Hiram would have to get a lawyer to figure out the land deal, but he imagined that Hiram would wind up with all of the Crowe land before much longer. There was really no one to worry about anymore other than the city gangsters, and Slocum did not think they would be any real trouble. There were only seven of them. Calvin Black had disappeared and Ernie was dead. If Agnes Glitch just sat tight there on the ranch, the only choice Slick Hannah would have would be to try to get her away from them, to attack the ranch. That had just been tried by a much bigger, if not tougher, force, and it hadn't worked. So Slocum figured that the best thing for him and the Newmans and Agnes Glitch to do was to just do nothing. Just sit and wait. Wait for the Hannah gang to make its move. Stay ready.

Slick called all of his boys together. They sat around a table in the saloon with a bottle of whiskey. Slick made sure that everyone had a glass filled. Then he stood up to address them. It was like a board meeting for some big corporation.

"Boys," he said, "things ain't been going so good for us out here. I know you all want to get back home as fast as we can. We've lost our allies out here, so now we're right back where we started. It's just us. But them allies wasn't worth much to start with. We can take these hayseeds without no help."

"That's right, boss," said Ziggie, scratching at his right leg.

"I said we're back where we started," Slick went on, "but that ain't quite true. We lost one man, but now we know where the woman is at. She's out there on that Newman ranch, and we know where that is too. She's got that Slocum guy and the Newman cowboys watching after her, so we'll have to deal with them."

"Boss," said Ziggie. "We're outnumbered. We'll have to have us a pretty good plan."

"Shut up, Ziggie. I'm talking. I'm talking, and I have a plan. One thing we know is that them cowboys keep a guard out by the road. We'll have to take care of him quiet like. We can't shoot him. They'll hear the shot, and then they'll be waiting for us."

He stopped and took a drink.

"All right," he said. "We take care of their guard quiet like, and then we sneak up to the house so they don't know we're there. Anyone we see, we conk them on the head. We keep quiet. We move in on the house and grab the woman. Then we either take her out with a knife or we take her with us and do it later on down the road somewheres. You all got that?"

"Boss?" said Ziggie

"What is it?"

"How do we get out there?"

"You're going down to the livery and rent a wagon and team. Bring it down here to the saloon, and we'll all load up in it and drive out there."

Slocum was still on the porch when Chief Johnson joined him there. Slocum gestured to a chair, and Johnson sat down. Slocum offered him a drink, but Johnson politely declined.

"Slocum," Johnson said, "how much longer do you think we'll have to wait for Hannah to make his move?"

"I don't think it will be long now," said Slocum. "He's

lost all his local help. He's got to do something right away."

"You think he'll come out here?"

"I don't think he's got much choice. He wants to get Agnes, and Agnes is here. She ain't likely to move while he's around, so he'll have to try to get her out. We'll be waiting."

"I sure hope you're right."

"Trust me, Chief," Slocum said.

"I do," said Agnes, stepping out the door.

"I didn't know you were listening to us," said Johnson, standing up politely.

"Please sit down, Chief," said Agnes, taking a chair for herself. "I wasn't listening at the door. I just walked up in time to hear Slocum say, 'Trust me.' That's all."

"I didn't mean to imply that you were eavesdropping," said Johnson.

"You holding up well enough?" Slocum asked.

"Yes," she said. "I'm all right. It's a little nerve-wracking, of course, to have this business still hanging over me, but I feel safe here. I'm all right."

"I think the whole business will be over and done with real soon now," Slocum said.

"I hope you're right," Agnes said. "I'm very grateful for all you've done for me. You and the Newmans." She looked at Chief Johnson, and she recalled the shooting she had seen in St. Louis. She thought about Slick Hannah and what he wanted to do to her. She wondered how much longer, for real, she would have to hide out on this cattle ranch in Kansas.

21

Ziggie had a hell of a time with the wagon. He turned too wide and had to back it up, but he did not know how to do that. After they stood on the sidewalk and laughed at him for a while, two cowboys helped him turn the wagon around. Then he whipped up the team, and it started running so fast that Ziggie almost fell over backward into the wagon bed. He managed to keep his seat though somehow, but he could not slow them down. The wagon raced on past the saloon. The main street was lined with laughing Kansans. Slick Hannah came out on the sidewalk in time to see Ziggie and the wagon disappear on the other end of town. He was humiliated by all the raucous laughter. At last he promised to pay a man with a horse to chase down the wagon and bring it back to the saloon.

"What about the driver?" the man said.

"I don't give a shit about him," said Slick. "Just bring me the wagon."

The man rode out of town fast, laughing as he went. Slick sat down in a chair that was there on the sidewalk and leaned back against the outside wall of the saloon. He took out a cigar and lit it, waiting impatiently. Finally, the man came back. He was driving the wagon, his horse tied on in back. There was no Ziggie. Slick paid the man, and the man walked back to his horse, still snickering. Slick went inside for a drink.

He turned to look over the remnants of his gang. "Can any of you assholes drive a wagon?" he asked. The assholes looked at one another, but no one responded. Slick had, of course, driven buggies in the city, so he figured that he could drive the wagon. "All right. All right," he said. "I'll drive the goddamned thing." He downed his drink and said, "Let's go."

Outside, the six gangsters climbed into the back of the wagon and Slick got up on the seat. "Hey, boss," said one. "What about Ziggie?"

"Fuck him," said Slick.

"Hey," said another, "here he comes."

Slick did not bother looking back. He started the horses moving slowly and headed out of town—in the right direction. Back behind them, Ziggie saw the wagon leaving. He started to run. The laughter on the street started all over again as the wagon rolled through town pursued by Ziggie, running as fast as he could go. Ziggie caught up at the far edge of town, and some of his cronies reached hands out to help him aboard the still-moving wagon. He fell down in the middle of the crowd, panting for breath.

"You okay, Ziggie?" one asked.

Still without looking back, Slick Hannah said, "Glad you could join us, Ziggie."

When he finally caught his breath, Ziggie managed to crawl forward. He climbed over onto the seat to sit beside

Slick. He was scratching his inner right thigh. "How come you was running off and leaving me like that?" he asked.

"You made me a laughingstock back there," Slick said. "The whole fucking town of goddamned hicks was laughing at me."

"I told you I couldn't handle a wagon."

They rode on in silence. Slick had a little trouble with the team, but he managed to keep it going, and at a pace that was reasonable. The wagon bounced along on the rough road though, and the ride for those in the back was anything but comfortable. Everyone was longing for the paved streets of St. Louis, and for the little one-horse buggies. All were wishing they were far away from the Wild West. One man took a bottle of whiskey out of his pocket, had a swig, and passed it around. Neither Slick nor Ziggie, both of whom were looking straight ahead and sulking, saw what was going on behind them.

In a short time, the six men in the back all had mild buzzes from the booze. "We're going to kill us some cowboys," one of them said.

"Yeah. We're going to wipe their ass out."

They all laughed.

"What's so goddamned funny back there?" said Slick.

"We're going to kill us some cowboys," said one of the men. "That's all."

"Well, quiet down before we reach the ranch," Slick ordered. He still had not turned his head and did not know that his men were slightly tipsy. A little farther on down the road, one of the men tossed the empty bottle out the back of the wagon.

"Are we getting close, boss?" one called out.

"Just a little farther," Slick answered.

The men all pulled out their guns and checked them. They were ready to do battle. Finally, Slick stopped the wagon. He climbed out and secured it there beside the road. The men were piling out the back of the wagon, still holding their weapons ready. Ziggie got down from the seat, still scratching. Slick gathered the men around.

"All right now," he said. "The gate's just down there. They got a sentry out, so whoever comes up on him first, knock him hard on the head. We don't want no unnecessary noise just yet. Let's go."

They crouched low and started sneaking up on the gate, but there was no sentry there. The sentry had heard the wagon coming, had heard it stop, and had managed to sneak a look at it. Then he had headed back for the ranch house with the word. When Slick and his men reached the gate, they all started poking their noses behind every brush and tree looking for the sentry.

"He's gotta be here," Slick said.

"If he's here, he knows we're here too by now," Ziggie said.

"All right. All right," said Slick. "Let's move on up to the house."

Still bent over, they started moving. They fought their way through brush and tangled bramble. Ziggie was constantly afraid that he would get into more of the mysterious bugs that had bitten him all over. Suddenly one of the men cried out, "Aaahh." Slick looked back furious.

"What the hell?" he said.

"A snake," the man said.

"Where?"

"He run off that way, but he was right here."

"They all probably know we're here by now," Slick said. "Be ready for anything."

But they were not ready for what happened next. Shots were fired. Cowboys whooped. The cattle that Slocum had ordered bunched up not far from the house came thundering toward the road, and of course, the Hannah gang was between the cattle and the road.

"What's that?" said Ziggie.

"It sounds like thunder," said one of the men.

Then they saw it, a mass of cattle rushing toward them, bellowing and braying, looking like monsters from hell, not at all like steaks, and sounding like a million demons. The frightened herd ran headlong into anything in its path. It sent up a huge cloud of dust as it surged forward. Some of the gangsters screamed. A couple of them stood up and fired into the thundering herd. One man climbed a tree. Ziggie hugged a tree trunk on the back side. The cattle trampled the two men who had foolishly stood their ground firing shots. They screamed hideously as they went down. Slick managed to run to one side and avoid the onslaught. He looked back in horror at what was happening. Then he looked toward the house.

This, he thought, might be his best chance. Surely everyone's eyes were focused on the stampeding cattle and what was happening to the men caught in front of them. He rushed on toward the house, going through the woods and the brush. He fought his way through the brambles, adding new cuts and scratches to those he already had. At last he broke loose. It was a clear space between him and the house. He stopped to study the lay of the land. No one seemed to be watching.

Back in the woods, cattle banged into trees and bounced

off, running into one another. Ziggie wished that he had gone up a sturdier tree, but he hadn't had time to think about that. Besides, he did not think he could have managed a tree with a thicker trunk. But this one swayed with his weight, and it swayed even worse when an animal banged into it as it hurried past.

He wondered if anyone down there was still alive. He wondered what he would do if he was the only one left alive. What would he do when it was all over? Wait until dark? Sit in the tree all day? Then climb down, and then what? He would be all alone out in this godforsaken wilderness. He would have to try to drive the wagon to the next town where he could buy a ticket on something, a stagecoach or a train.

His balls itched, and he held on tight with one hand while he scratched furiously at them with the other. Then he realized that he had dropped his gun in his flight to safety. He would really be in trouble if he ran into anyone without his gun. He wondered again if all his pals were dead. He wondered about Slick. Then a huge bull ran into the tree, and Ziggie lost his grip. He screamed as he fell, crashing into and through several tree branches on the trip back down to the ground. He tried desperately to grab on to something. Then he bounced on the backs of several moving animals before he hit the ground. His screams as the sharp hooves trounced him were hideous to hear.

At last the cattle stopped running. They moved around nervously, lowing, slowly settling down. There was no other movement though. The men at the house stared out to see if anyone would move, but no one did. "The cattle got them all," said Hiram.

"It looks that way," Slocum said.

"Aubrey," said Hiram, "let's get the cattle rounded up and back out on the pasture where they belong."

"Yes, sir," said Aubrey.

Johnson went in the house to look for Agnes. "Miss Glitch?" he called.

She came out of the kitchen. "I'm here," she said.

"They just wiped out the Hannah gang."

"Oh, thank goodness."

"Will you be going back to St. Louis?"

"Soon. In a day or so."

"Maybe you'll write me a statement about what you saw in St. Louis before I leave. I'll be headed back as soon as I can get a train or a stage. Whatever leaves first."

"I'll write you a statement," she said.

"Thank you. I don't think there'll be any need for you to show up at a hearing or anything like that. With my word that Hannah got killed and your word about what he did, the case will be closed. One good thing about all this is that the days of the Hannah gang in St. Louis are over. If there's anyone left back there who was involved in it, they'll all fall apart."

"I'm glad of that," she said. "Chief, would you like some coffee?"

"I think I'd like a drink."

"I'll just get you one."

She walked past him to the bar in the living room, and just as she did, Slick Hannah stepped through the back door. He saw Agnes, and he saw Chief Johnson standing between him and Agnes, both of them with their backs to him. He could kill them both and get the hell out of there. He raised his gun and pointed it at Johnson's back.

Silly Sally, who had been hiding in a bedroom, stepped

out just then. She took in the situation immediately. "Look out," she screamed. Slick turned toward the new noise and fired instinctively. His bullet hit Silly Sally in the right shoulder. She screamed and fell down. Johnson pulled out his revolver and whirled at the same time, firing into Slick Hannah's chest. Slick jerked and staggered. He tried to hold up his gun, but fell against the wall. Johnson fired again, this time catching Slick right in the heart. Slick slid down the wall, leaving a smear of blood behind him. He stopped in a sitting position, his head dangling on his chest. Johnson ran over to him to make sure he was dead. Agnes ran to Silly Sally.

"Am I going to die?" Silly Sally asked.

"Of course not," said Agnes.

Johnson was there by then. He took a quick look at the wound.

"I think you'll be all right," he said.

Maudie came in then, and they carried Silly Sally to a bed where Maudie, with Agnes's help, dressed the wound. Having heard the shots, Hiram and Slocum came in. They hauled the body outside. Then they walked over the land, locating all the remains they could find. At last they concluded that the fight was over. They had won.

There were legal problems to hash out. Agnes wrote her statement out for Johnson. He took it and thanked her kindly. Over the next few days, county officials were consulted who determined somehow that Hiram Newman owned the entire Crowe ranch, not just that portion that Crowe had stolen from him, and that Silly Sally owned the saloon in town unless Calvin Black were to show up again. Then they would reconsider. They would also consider filing charges against Black for his involvement with the Slick Hannah gang.

With everything settled, more or less, to everyone's satisfaction, Johnson announced that he would return to St. Louis. Agnes said that she might just as well go along at the same time. Aubrey Newman drove them both to town in a wagon, and Slocum went along on his Appaloosa. They arrived just in time to catch the stage to Baxter Springs. When the stage rolled out with Johnson and Agnes aboard, Slocum rode alongside once again. Baxter Springs was, after all, his jumping-off point for the trip through Indian Territory and on down into Texas. He had not forgotten that goal. The ride to Baxter Springs was uneventful. They arrived in the middle of the afternoon.

Checking on the train schedule, they found that they would have to spend a night in town and catch the early-morning train out. The three of them went together for a meal. Then Johnson got himself a hotel room, and Agnes did the same. Saying good night, Johnson mounted the stairs to go to his room. Agnes looked at Slocum. This might be the last night she would ever see him.

"Would you like to come up?" she asked him.

22

Inside the hotel room, Agnes fell into Slocum's arms. He held her tightly. "Slocum," she said, "this is probably the last time we'll ever see each other."

"Don't say that," he said. "You never know about these things."

She leaned back and looked up into his eyes. He bent forward and kissed her on the lips. It was a long and lingering kiss. At last, Agnes broke away and walked over to the bed. She turned to face Slocum and started undoing her dress. She had a sly smile on her beautiful face. Slocum returned the smile and walked over to her, pulling off his shirt. Soon they were both naked, standing, facing each other. They embraced again, and this time, feeling the closeness of her naked body, Slocum felt his tool begin to rise. Agnes felt it as well as it nudged against her belly.

She turned and pulled the bedclothes down, then crawled in on her hands and knees, her lovely round ass cheeks showing themselves to Slocum as she did so. When she reached the middle of the bed, she flopped over onto her back, spreading her legs wide apart. Slocum moved in quickly, placing himself on top of her and between her legs. He kissed her again on the lips, and their tongues began dueling with each other. Slocum's rod was throbbing.

Agnes reached down with both hands to guide it into her ready slit. As soon as he felt it in place, Slocum thrust downward, driving his tool all the way into her. "Oh, Slocum," she said. "That's good. That's good." He humped and thrust, in and out, faster and faster, harder and harder. "Oh, oh," she moaned.

"Ahhh," Slocum growled. Each time he drove himself into her, their bodies came together with a loud *slap*. She wrapped her legs around his waist and locked her ankles, holding him in a tight grip. Her nails scratched his back. He drove himself in and out.

At last, Slocum slowed his pace. He was panting, she was panting, and they both were sweating heavily, their bodies sliding on each other. Slocum stopped humping, grabbed Agnes tightly, and rolled over onto his back with her on top. She drew her knees up under her, sitting hard on him, glorying in the feeling of his thick tool in her squishy cunt. She started sliding her ass back and forth along the middle of his body, sliding in the cunt juice and sweat.

She moved faster and faster, and Slocum did not have to do anything other than lie there and enjoy it. She moaned louder as she moved faster, then with a loud groan, she stopped her motions and fell forward, her breasts pressing against his chest, her lips finding his. "Oh, God," she said, "that was good." She took a few deep breaths, and then she sat up again. Again she started rocking back and forth. This time it did not take her as long to reach her climax, and she fell down again with an even louder cry of pleasure. At last, she could take no more, and she stopped, sitting up, looking down on Slocum with pleasure written on her face. His tool was still rigid inside her. She backed off and moved down, taking it into her mouth. She bounced her head up and down, slurping, driving Slocum nearly mad. He felt the pressure build and knew that he was about to come. His groan told her the same thing. She bounced faster. Then Slocum shot forth into her mouth again and again. When he was done at last, she lay her head on his thigh, holding the rod as it wilted, smiling. They went to sleep like that.

In the morning, Agnes and Slocum met Johnson for breakfast. They had a leisurely meal and Slocum and Johnson ordered more coffee. Agnes refused more coffee, saying she wanted to do a little shopping before getting on the train. She excused herself and left the eatery.

"Slocum," said Johnson, "I want to tell you something."

"I'm listening," Slocum said.

"I just want to thank you for all your help on this case. I'm sure as hell glad you were around."

"It wasn't much," Slocum said. "The Newmans did as much as I did."

"You can be modest if you want to," said Johnson, "but you were a big help, and I'm grateful. I'm sure that Miss Glitch is too."

At his hotel window, Calvin Black was watching for any sign of the Slick Hannah gang when he saw Agnes going down the sidewalk alone. His heart suddenly beat faster. He could scarcely believe his good fortune. This was his big chance. He could catch her and deliver her to Slick

Hannah, and that would save him from Slick's wrath. He could simply say that he had gotten wind of where she was really hiding and gone after her. Strike when the iron was hot. He would say that he was sorry for having seemed to have run out on Slick, but he had to move fast. Hannah would be so relieved at getting his hands on the gal, he would forget his anger at having been abandoned. It was perfect.

Black grabbed his coat and hat and hurried outside. Agnes was just across the street, headed for the hotel. He ran. He came up behind her and grabbed her by the shoulders, pulling her into the narrow space between two buildings, shoving her against the wall and putting a hand over her mouth. Her eyes were wide. Black saw fear there, and he enjoyed it.

Agnes fumbled with her purse. She got it opened and put her right hand inside, gripping the handle of the Merwin and Hulbert revolver she had bought earlier in this very town. Black was totally unaware of what she had done. Pressing the muzzle of the revolver, still hidden inside her purse, against Black's chest, she pulled the trigger. The sound of the blast was muffled somewhat, but it still roared in that narrow space. Black's face registered a horrible surprise. His eyes opened wide, his mouth dropped open, and his hand slid from her mouth. He staggered back, his knees buckling, and he fell dead.

"Was that a shot?" said Johnson.

"Sounded like it," Slocum said.

"I wonder what's going on."

"Well, let's go check it out."

They got up, and Johnson paid the bill. Outside, they

saw a small crowd gathering across the street. They walked over and craned their necks. Slocum was the first to see Agnes. A sheriff had a hand on one of her arms. He couldn't hear what was being said until the sheriff said loudly, "All right, boys, spread out and give us room."

The crowd parted and the sheriff and Agnes walked through the space. The sheriff spoke over his shoulder, "A couple of you men get the stiff down to the undertaker's. Come along, miss."

"What's happened here?" said Slocum.

"I killed Calvin Black," Agnes said.

Johnson and Slocum fell in step with the sheriff and Agnes and walked to the sheriff's office with them. As the sheriff ushered Agnes inside, he turned to face the two men.

"What's your interest here?" he said.

Johnson pulled out his identification and showed it to the sheriff. "I'm a police chief from St. Louis," he said.

"I'm a friend," said Slocum.

"I believe we have information relevant to this matter," Johnson said.

"Well, come on in," said the sheriff.

Inside, the sheriff got everyone seated. "Here's what I found," he said. "This lady was standing over a dead man. The man was shot, and she was holding a gun. The dead man was unarmed. It seems pretty clear to me. Now what do you have to say?"

"He grabbed me and pulled me in between the buildings," Agnes said. "I shot him."

"Sheriff," said Johnson, "I followed this woman and a notorious gang of criminals from St. Louis. The criminals were following her. She was a witness to a murder in St. Louis, and she fled for her life, but the gang followed her.

When they got out here, they enlisted that man Black to help them find her. We killed all the gang members in a fight over near Coffeyville, but Black had no way of knowing that. He must have grabbed her, thinking that he would turn her over to Slick Hannah and be rewarded for his trouble."

"That's about the size of it," said Slocum.

The sheriff tended to believe the tale, but he said there would have to be an inquest. He thought he could get it together quickly, and he did. The next afternoon the inquest found that there was no cause to hold Agnes, no need for a trial. She was dismissed. Johnson and Agnes were able to get tickets on a train later that same afternoon, and saying fond farewells to Slocum, they boarded the train. Slocum stood and watched it go. When it was out of sight, he mounted his Appaloosa and started riding south, resuming his long-delayed trip to Texas.

Watch for

SLOCUM AND THE HIGH-GRADERS

341st novel in the exciting SLOCUM series from Jove

Coming in July!